MARTIN HAYES

JIM BOSWELL

# Project Luna 1947

 Published by Markosia Enterprises, PO BOX 3477, Barnet, Hertfordshire, EN5 9HN. FIRST PRINTING, February2013. Harry Markos, Director.

ISBN: 978-1-909276-02-4

# Project Luna 1947

Written by
MARTIN HAYES

Art & Letters by
JIM BOSWELL

For Markosia Enterprises Ltd

HARRY MARKOS
Publisher & Managing Partner

IAN SHARMAN ■ GM JORDAN ■ ANDY BRIGGS
Group Editors

*Dedicated to my cousin Ben Martin - a huge supporter of my work on this book - who sadly passed away in 2012 before he had the chance to read the final pages.*

**Jim Boswell**

JUNE 24TH 1947.

KENNETH ARNOLD SEES SOMETHING EXCEEDINGLY STRANGE FLY PAST THE WING OF HIS CALLAIR A-2.

JUNE 30TH, JUST OUTSIDE OF MANCHESTER.
AND YOU'VE VERIFIED IT... THE SIGNAL REPEATS ITSELF?
I'VE BEEN MONITORING THE FREQUENCY FOR OVER TWENTY MINUTES. IT PULSES ONCE EVERY SEVENTEEN SECONDS.
I DON'T UNDERSTAND IT, THE REPETITION, THE LOCATION. I MEAN, IT'S *INCREDIBLE*.
DR. ROYCE, WHAT DO WE DO NOW? SHOULDN'T WE TELL SOMEBODY ABOUT THIS?

F7J
2P36
6E1T
F6
6EQ9U17W0L8J265
F26
bloody hell!
I SUPPOSE SO. BUT WHO DO WE REPORT IT TO?
WHO WOULD EVEN BELIEVE US?

JULY 7TH.
ROSWELL, NEW MEXICO.
HOW LONG SINCE YOU CALLED THE SHERIFF?
'BOUT FORTY-FIVE MINUTES, I GUESS.
SO HE'LL BE HERE SOON THEN?
FIGURE. SAID HE WAS GONNA BRING SOME OF THEM SOLDIER TYPES FROM THE BASE ALONG WITH HIM.
HE SOUNDED LIKE HE DONE MESSED HIS PANTS WHEN I TOLD HIM WHAT IT WAS THAT WE FOUND OUT HERE.
WELL, I CAN'T SAY THAT I BLAME HIM FOR THAT.
YOU THINK THIS IS THE SAME TYPE A'THING THAT FELLA IN WASHINGTON SAW LAST MONTH?
I SURE DO HOPE SO. HE AIN'T DOING TOO BAD OFF IT, BEEN ON TV, IN THE PAPERS, MUST BE MAKING A FORTUNE.

HEY MATT, I THINK WE SHOULD KEEP CLEAR 'TILL THE SHERIFF GETS HERE.
SHUSH, NOW. I'M JUST TAKING A LOOK. COULD BE MADE OUTA GOLD OR ANYTHING. YOU WANT THE ARMY NABBING THIS THING AND SQUIRLING IT AWAY FOR THEMSELVES?
HELL, I BET WE DON'T GET SO MUCH AS A FINDER'S FEE.
CLICK
PSHHHHHHHHH
- AHUCG -
NNNNJEEESUS
THLOOOP
AAAAAAAAAAA!
HLUGCKKKKKK...

HELP ME!
AHHH... SWEET JESUS... PLEASE!
1-3R52
BLAM
BLAM

LONDON, JULY 20TH.
YES SIR. YES, I AM AWARE OF THE TREATY.
YES, HE'S AT MY DOOR NOW... I'LL GET RIGHT BACK TO YOU. GOODBYE SIR.
COME IN DR. ROYCE. I'M SO SORRY TO HAVE KEPT YOU WAITING.
THANK YOU, SIR.
HOW NICE TO FINALLY MEET YOU.
IT'S A GREAT HONOUR TO MEET YOU, SIR.
PLEASE DR. ROYCE. TAKE A SEAT, WILL YOU.
WELL NOW, I'VE HAD A CHANCE TO LOOK OVER YOUR FINDINGS. THEY ARE MOST INTERESTING.
YES SIR. I HAVE FURTHER READOUTS HERE, FROM LAST WEEK AND --
OH, THAT WON'T BE NECESSARY.
EVER SINCE THIS WAS BROUGHT TO MY ATTENTION WE HAVE BEEN GOING THROUGH YOUR OFFICES WHEN YOU LEAVE FOR THE NIGHT.
B-B-BUT --

OH, IT WAS NOTHING PERSONAL, I ASSURE YOU, DR. ROYCE. IT'S JUST THE WAY WE DO THINGS AROUND HERE.
JOLLY GOOD LUCK THAT YOUR BOSS AND I WERE AT ETON TOGETHER. ALWAYS BEST TO KEEP THIS KIND OF THING HUSH-HUSH.
AND I TRUST THAT YOU AND YOUR COLLEAGUE HAVE MENTIONED THIS TO NO ONE ELSE?
OH NO, OF COURSE NOT. I --
GOOD MAN! GOOD MAN! THIS COULD ALL GET RATHER STICKY BEFORE IT'S THROUGH. ABOVE TOP SECRET AND ALL THAT...
WOULDN'T WANT ANY OF THOSE BLASTED TABLOIDS GETTING HOLD OF IT, WOULD WE?
NOW, PERHAPS YOU CAN EXPLAIN ALL THIS TO ME. IT'S NOT REALLY MY FIELD, YOU KNOW.
YES SIR. WELL, IT'S THE LONG LINE OF DIGITS. THEY ARE WHAT IS SO UNUSUAL, SO UNBELIEVABLE.
OH YES, AND WHY SO?
WELL SIR, IT'S A SIGNAL. NOT A VERY POWERFUL ONE BUT A SIGNAL NONETHELESS.
AND IT COMES FROM--
THE MOON, SIR. IT COMES FROM THE MOON.
AS TO WHAT IT IS, I JUST DON'T KNOW. PERHAPS IT'S A COMMUNICATION DEVICE OF SOME KIND. OR A HOMING BEACON. WE MAY EVEN BE EXPERIENCING THE COSMIC EQUIVALENT OF A CROSSED LINE ON A TELEPHONE.

COMMUNICATION! CROSSED LINES! THEN YOU MEAN IT DEFINITELY DISPLAYS SOME SORT OF INTELLIGENCE?
YES SIR. IT PULSES ONCE EVERY SEVENTEEN SECONDS. THAT WOULD INDICATE INTELLIGENT DESIGN.
GOOD LORD!
AH, SAMANTHA. THANK YOU EVER SO MUCH.
ALTHOUGH, I FEAR THAT DR. ROYCE SHAN'T BE STAYING FOR TEA.
ON BEHALF OF THE GOVERNMENT, I WOULD LIKE TO THANK YOU DR. ROYCE. YOU HAVE BEEN MOST HELPFUL.
THANK YOU, SIR.
MOST HELPFUL INDEED.
THANK YOU, MY DEAR.
IT'S ME SIR... YES, IT IS AS WE FEARED. YES SIR, IT WOULD APPEAR THAT IT IS CONNECTED TO THE RECENT ACTIVITY.
YES SIR... THE PROVIDENCE TREATY.
YES, I WILL MEET WITH THEM EARLY NEXT WEEK.
GOODBYE PRIME MINISTER.

SURREY, JULY 29TH.
LOVELY WEATHER.
YES, MR. SPEARS. THE SUMMER HAS BEEN EXTREMELY PLEASANT THIS YEAR.
MY WIFE TAKES CARE OF THE GARDEN. SHE'S DONE A WONDERFUL JOB WITH IT.
YES, SHE CERTAINLY HAS.
I DO HOPE YOU ALL LIKE TEA.
IT'S A GREAT PLEASURE TO FINALLY MEET YOU ALL, GENTLEMEN.
ALLOW ME TO MAKE THE FORMAL INTRODUCTIONS.
MR. SPEARS, HEAD OF THE UNITED STATES' CENTRAL INTELLIGENCE AGENCY, WHICH WAS RECENTLY FOUNDED TO LOOK INTO THIS SITUATION.
MR. DE BLANCHFORT, CHIEF OF THE S.D.E.C.E. - THE FRENCH SECRET SERVICE.
AND GENERAL MELNIKOV, HEAD OF THE K.G.B.

I HAVE ASKED YOU HERE BECAUSE WE MUST FULFILL A PACT WHICH OUR LEADERS MADE OVER TWO YEARS AGO.
YOU MEAN... *PROVIDENCE!*

YES. WE HAVE A SITUATION HERE THAT COULD BE *EXTREMELY DANGEROUS* FOR ALL OUR NATIONS.
TELL ME MR. JACKINGTON, WHY SHOULD MY COUNTRY HELP ITS *CAPITALIST OPPRESSORS* IN THIS MATTER?

BECAUSE EVEN BEHIND THE IRON CURTAIN, I STILL THINK A *GENTLEMAN'S AGREEMENT* SHOULD BE HONORED.
*AGREED.*
*OUI.*

YOU KNOW AS WELL AS I DO THAT IN FEBRUARY OF *1945* OUR LEADERS MET IN PROVIDENCE, RHODE ISLAND WHILE THOSE *LOOK-ALIKES* WERE PRATTLING AWAY IN *YALTA*. YOU ALSO KNOW THEY AGREED THAT IF THE WORLD WAS EVER THREATENED AGAIN --
THEN ALL FOUR OF OUR *GREAT NATIONS* WOULD POOL THEIR RESOURCES TO COMBAT THAT THREAT.

*YES, YES,* VERY WELL, TELL US OF *BRITAIN'S* PROBLEM.
IT'S NOT JUST OUR PROBLEM, GENERAL MELNIKOV. THIS SITUATION COULD AFFECT EVERY LAST ORGANISM ON THE PLANET.

MR. SPEARS, PERHAPS IF YOU WERE TO BEGIN --

WHAT I'M ABOUT TO TELL YOU IS ***ABOVE TOP SECRET.*** IF THE SITUATION WASN'T SO DIRE, I WOULD PROBABLY BE SHOT AS A TRAITOR FOR EVEN DISCUSSING THIS WITH YOU.
FOR THE LAST SIX MONTHS PEOPLE FROM ALL OVER THE U.S, FROM PORTLAND, MAINE TO PORTLAND, OREGON, HAVE BEEN REPORTING SIGHTINGS OF STRANGE LIGHTS AND DISC-SHAPED OBJECTS IN THE SKY.

OBVIOUSLY, THE GOVERNMENT TOOK AN INTEREST, ESPECIALLY AFTER THE FOO-FIGHTER SIGHTINGS DURING THE WAR. BUT TO BE HONEST, WE THOUGHT IT WAS A LOAD OF BALONEY.

UNTIL THREE WEEKS AGO. YOU SEE --
***WE FOUND ONE.***

THE OCCUPANT OF THE DISC WAS STILL ALIVE. IT WAS INCREDIBLY HOSTILE SO OUR TROOPS HAD NO CHOICE BUT TO ELIMINATE IT.
IT TOOK TWENTY-EIGHT BULLETS TO PUT IT DOWN.

THE CRAFT IS DAMAGED BUT FUNCTIONAL.

A WELL-PLACED MOLE IN THE KREMLIN HAS ALREADY INFORMED US THAT YOU HAVE HAD YOUR OWN SIGHTINGS AND ENCOUNTERS.

ST. PETERSBURG, WASN'T IT? AND VLADIVOSTOK?

AND LAST MONTH'S SIGHTING AT LYON.

THIS IS OUTRAGEOUS! HOW DO YOU KNOW THESE THINGS? HOW DARE YOU SPY ON THE GREAT SOV--

PLEASE, GENERAL MELNIKOV.
PLEASE, JUST ONE MORE MINUTE OF YOUR TIME.

I APOLOGIZE FOR ANY DISTRESS MR. SPEARS MAY HAVE CAUSED, BUT IT WAS ESSENTIAL THAT WE CUT THROUGH ALL THE RED TAPE AND BUREAUCRATIC OBFUSCATION.
WE HAVE ALL HAD RECENT ENCOUNTERS WITH THESE STRANGE VISITORS.

AND THANKS TO A COUPLE OF RATHER BOOKISH ENGLISH ASTRONOMERS, WE MAY JUST HAVE DISCOVERED WHERE THEY ARE COMING FROM.

THAT IS WHY I HAVE CALLED EACH OF YOU HERE TODAY. THAT IS WHY WE MUST FULFILL THE *PROVIDENCE TREATY*.
GENTLEMEN, *WE ARE GOING TO THE MOON.*

LONDON.
TWO PINTS OF BITTER PLEASE, MATE.
COMING UP.
WELL MY LOVELY, HOW MUCH IS THE GOING RATE THEN?
BROWN?
SQUADRON LEADER WILLIAM FITZWILLIAM BROWN?

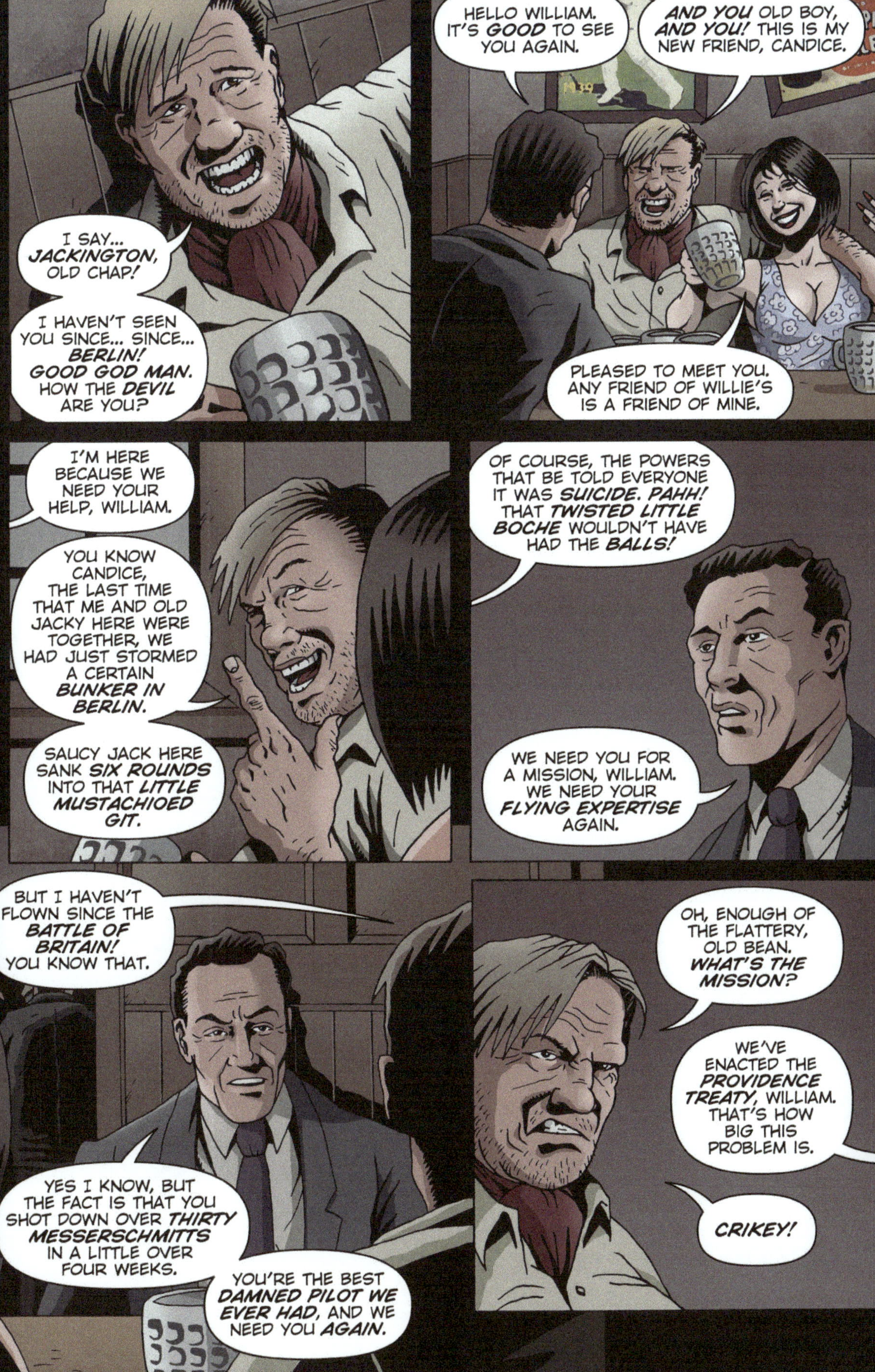
I SAY... JACKINGTON, OLD CHAP!
I HAVEN'T SEEN YOU SINCE... SINCE... BERLIN! GOOD GOD MAN. HOW THE DEVIL ARE YOU?
HELLO WILLIAM. IT'S GOOD TO SEE YOU AGAIN.
AND YOU OLD BOY, AND YOU! THIS IS MY NEW FRIEND, CANDICE.
PLEASED TO MEET YOU. ANY FRIEND OF WILLIE'S IS A FRIEND OF MINE.
I'M HERE BECAUSE WE NEED YOUR HELP, WILLIAM.
YOU KNOW CANDICE, THE LAST TIME THAT ME AND OLD JACKY HERE WERE TOGETHER, WE HAD JUST STORMED A CERTAIN BUNKER IN BERLIN.
SAUCY JACK HERE SANK SIX ROUNDS INTO THAT LITTLE MUSTACHIOED GIT.
OF COURSE, THE POWERS THAT BE TOLD EVERYONE IT WAS SUICIDE. PAHH! THAT TWISTED LITTLE BOCHE WOULDN'T HAVE HAD THE BALLS!
WE NEED YOU FOR A MISSION, WILLIAM. WE NEED YOUR FLYING EXPERTISE AGAIN.
BUT I HAVEN'T FLOWN SINCE THE BATTLE OF BRITAIN! YOU KNOW THAT.
YES I KNOW, BUT THE FACT IS THAT YOU SHOT DOWN OVER THIRTY MESSERSCHMITTS IN A LITTLE OVER FOUR WEEKS.
YOU'RE THE BEST DAMNED PILOT WE EVER HAD, AND WE NEED YOU AGAIN.
OH, ENOUGH OF THE FLATTERY, OLD BEAN. WHAT'S THE MISSION?
WE'VE ENACTED THE PROVIDENCE TREATY, WILLIAM. THAT'S HOW BIG THIS PROBLEM IS.
CRIKEY!

NEW MEXICO.
AND YOU SAY HE'S GOOD?
YES, MR. SPEARS. HE'S THE BEST.
HE'S THE ONLY MAN WE HAVE THAT CAN HANDLE THE... OUR LATEST... ACQUISITION, SIR.
HE SOUNDS IDEAL. I READ HIS FILE ON THE WAY HERE, SEEMS LIKE THE PERFECT MAN FOR THE JOB.
THERE ISN'T A MAN ON THIS BASE WHO WOULDN'T TRUST CAPTAIN WELLES WITH HIS LIFE.
GREAT LANDING, CAPTAIN WELLES.
THANK YOU, SIR. SHE TAKES A LITTLE WHILE TO GET USED TO, BUT I THINK I'M GETTING THE HANG OF HER.
LOOK HARRY, I WON'T BEAT AROUND THE BUSH. I'VE GOT A SPECIAL MISSION AND I'D LIKE YOU ON BOARD. YOU'LL BE WORKING WITH SPECIALISTS FROM OTHER COUNTRIES --
AND THERE'LL BE A LOT OF TRAVEL INVOLVED.
IF YOU THINK I CAN HELP, SIR, THEN I'M IN. WHERE WILL WE BE TRAVELING TO?
OH, YOU'LL FIND OUT SOON ENOUGH.

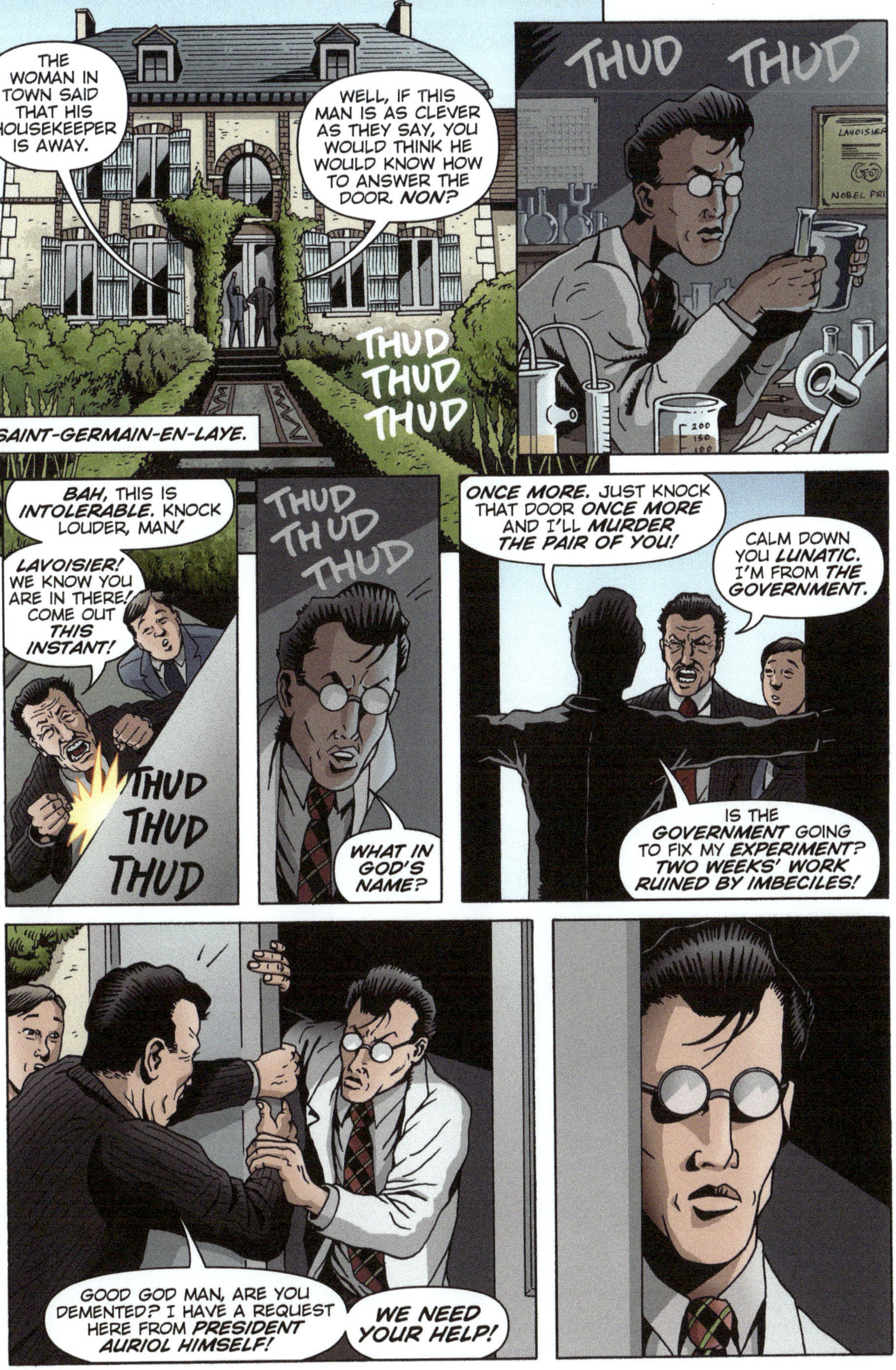

THE WOMAN IN TOWN SAID THAT HIS HOUSEKEEPER IS AWAY.
WELL, IF THIS MAN IS AS CLEVER AS THEY SAY, YOU WOULD THINK HE WOULD KNOW HOW TO ANSWER THE DOOR. *NON?*
THUD THUD THUD
SAINT-GERMAIN-EN-LAYE.

THUD THUD

*BAH*, THIS IS *INTOLERABLE*. KNOCK LOUDER, MAN!
*LAVOISIER!* WE KNOW YOU ARE IN THERE! COME OUT *THIS INSTANT!*
THUD THUD THUD

THUD THUD THUD
*WHAT IN GOD'S NAME?*

*ONCE MORE.* JUST KNOCK THAT DOOR *ONCE MORE* AND I'LL *MURDER THE PAIR OF YOU!*
CALM DOWN YOU *LUNATIC.* I'M FROM *THE GOVERNMENT.*
IS THE *GOVERNMENT* GOING TO FIX MY *EXPERIMENT? TWO WEEKS' WORK RUINED BY IMBECILES!*

Comrade Grusov is a valued Party Member. When he was seven years old he informed the K.G.B. that his neighbour had

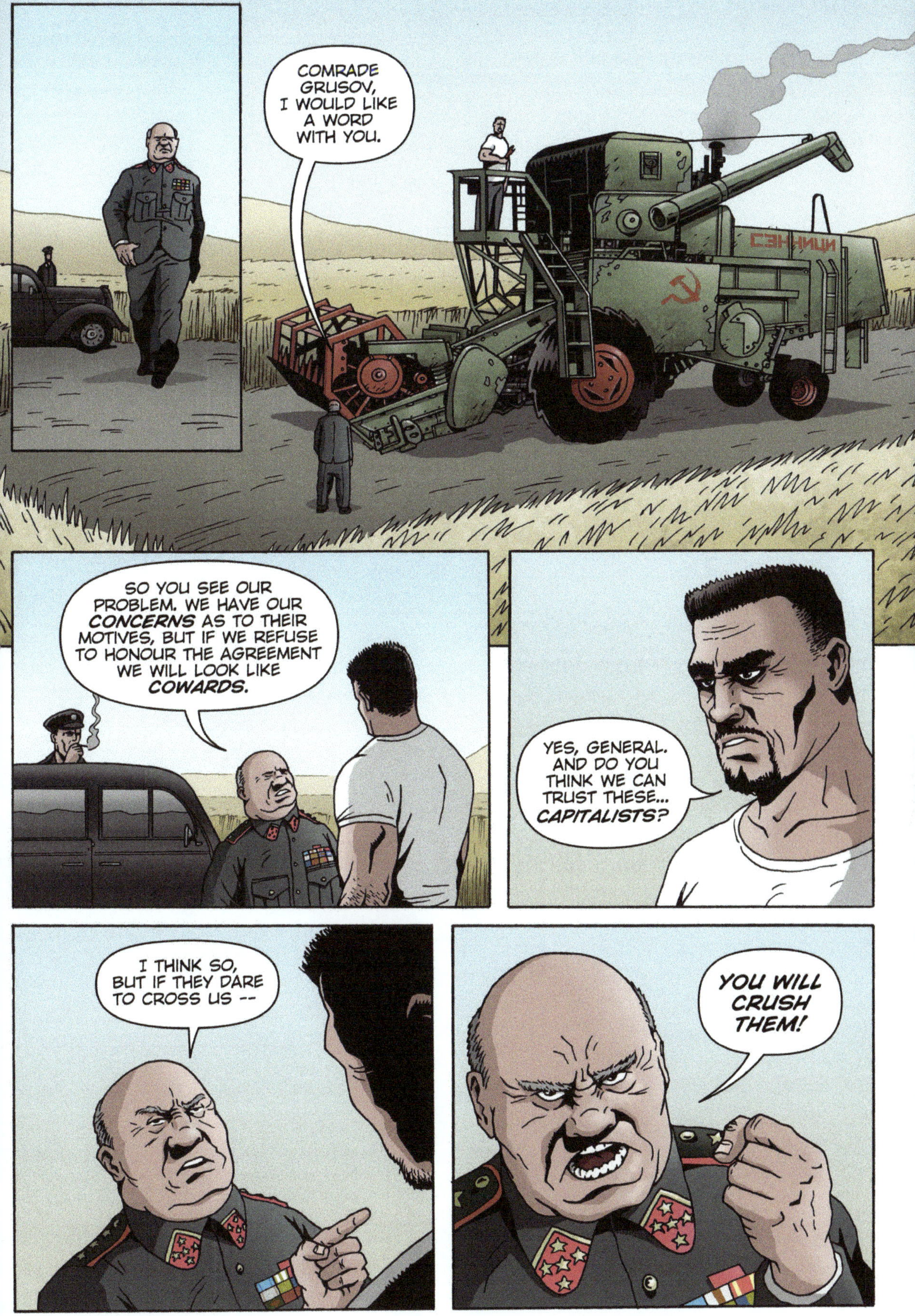

COMRADE GRUSOV, I WOULD LIKE A WORD WITH YOU.

SO YOU SEE OUR PROBLEM. WE HAVE OUR ***CONCERNS*** AS TO THEIR MOTIVES, BUT IF WE REFUSE TO HONOUR THE AGREEMENT WE WILL LOOK LIKE ***COWARDS.***

YES, GENERAL. AND DO YOU THINK WE CAN TRUST THESE... ***CAPITALISTS?***

HEY THERE SLEEPY HEAD.

PROMISE US SOMETHING.
WHAT?
THAT YOU'LL COME BACK.

OHH WILLIAM, DO YOU *HAVE* TO GO?
CAN'T YOU STAY FOR A *LITTLE LONGER?*
SORRY MY LOVELY, CAN'T BE HELPED. *KING AND COUNTRY AND ALL THAT.*
HERE, TAKE AN EXTRA *FIVER*. BUY YOURSELF A NEW FROCK.

AUGUST 22ND, LONDON.
YES SIR, EVERYTHING IS RUNNING SMOOTHLY.
THEY HAVE ALREADY LEFT. I'M TOLD THEY SHOULD ALL ARRIVE HERE BY NEXT TUESDAY AT THE LATEST.
YES... THE SECRET CENTER.
Scotland
NORTH ATLANTIC OCEAN
IRELAND
UNITED KINGDOM
Wales
England
YES SIR, VERY REMOTE. I'M TOLD THAT EVEN THE LOCALS HAVE NO IDEA IT'S THERE.
THEY THINK IT'S SOME KIND OF SHEEP FARM.

SEPTEMBER 10TH: SOMEWHERE IN THE SCOTTISH HIGHLANDS.
THE SECRET CENTRE.
NO ENTRY
BEYOND THIS POINT
AGRICULTURAL
TESTING SITE
POSSIBLE RISK OF
CONTAMINATION
IT JUST SEEMS STRANGE; THEY'VE BOTH SENT THEIR BEST MEN, SO WHY WOULDN'T THE RUSSIANS AND THE FRENCH WANT THEIR CONSULS TO BE HERE?
OHH, IT'S JUST THE USUAL DIPLOMATIC BACKSIDE COVERING, I SHOULD THINK.
IF THIS ALL GOES BELLY-UP THEY'LL PROBABLY CLAIM THAT THE MEN THEY SENT WERE DEFECTORS AND THAT THIS WAS ALL SOME BRITISH-AMERICAN PLOT.
AND THE MEN HAVEN'T BEEN INTRODUCED YET?
I BELIEVE THAT CAPTAIN WELLES AND SQUADRON LEADER BROWN MET YESTERDAY. GRUSOV AND LAVOISIER ARRIVED LATE LAST NIGHT - THERE WAS NO TIME FOR INTRODUCTIONS.

YES, I REMEMBER ANDERSON, *HELL OF A PILOT*. HE WAS STATIONED WITH ME AT TANGMERE FOR A WHILE.
HE TALKED ABOUT YOU ALL THE TIME ONCE HE GOT HOME.

AND *HOW THE HELL* IS THE OLD BOY?
HE'S GOOD, GOT MARRIED TO A CABARET SINGER, LIVES IN MICHIGAN NOW, HAS TWO BEAUTIFUL DAUGHTERS.
I'M GLAD, SUCH A NICE CHAP.

WELL, IT LOOKS LIKE ALL OF OUR TEAM HAS FINALLY ARRIVED.
I THINK IT'S TIME YOU FELLAS WERE FORMALLY INTRODUCED.

PROFESSOR VLADIMIR GRUSOV, DR. JACQUES LAVOISIER, PLEASE MEET...

...CAPTAIN HARRY WELLES AND SQUADRON LEADER WILLIAM FITZWILLIAM BROWN.
*BLOODY HELL! BRITS, YANKS,* NOW *FROGS* AND *RUSKIES.*
WHO ARE WE GOING TO BUNK UP WITH NEXT SPEARS? *THE BLOODY GERMANS?!!*

COME NOW GENTLEMEN, OUR NATIONS NEED US. I'M SURE WE CAN PUT OUR DIFFERENCES ASIDE.
TIME *IS* AN ISSUE AFTER ALL.
IT WOULD APPEAR WE HAVE LITTLE CHOICE.

WHAT'S YOUR GAME, SPEARS? I DIDN'T SIGN UP TO WORK WITH BLOODY ***COMMUNISTS*** AND ***SURRENDER MONKEYS.***

***WHO DO YOU THINK YOU ARE TO CALL ME SUCH NAMES?***
I'LL HAVE YOU KNOW I FOUGHT IN ***THE RESISTANCE.***

OHH COME ON, OLD BEAN. I HARDLY THINK THAT HIDING IN A ***WARDROBE*** CAN BE CALLED "RESISTING".

***GENTLEMEN, PLEASE.*** WE'RE SUPPOSED TO BE PROFESSIONALS.

I HAVE SOMETHING TO SHOW YOU ALL.
SOMETHING WHICH MIGHT STOP ALL THIS CHILDISH BICKERING.

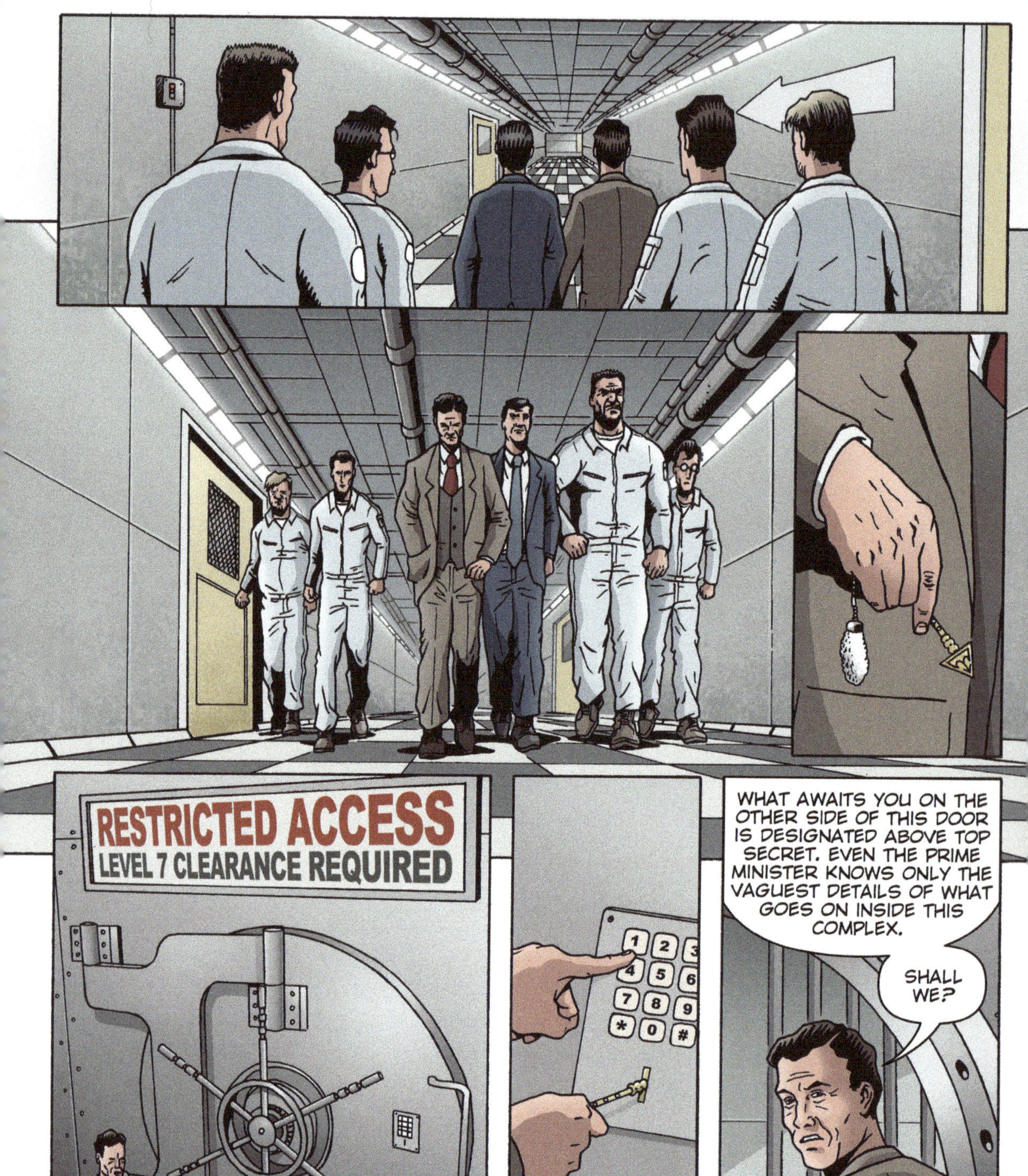
RESTRICTED ACCESS
LEVEL 7 CLEARANCE REQUIRED
HERE WE ARE.
1 2 3
4 5 6
7 8 9
* 0 #
WHAT AWAITS YOU ON THE OTHER SIDE OF THIS DOOR IS DESIGNATED ABOVE TOP SECRET. EVEN THE PRIME MINISTER KNOWS ONLY THE VAGUEST DETAILS OF WHAT GOES ON INSIDE THIS COMPLEX.
SHALL WE?

YE GODS!
GENTLEMEN, ALLOW ME TO INTRODUCE YOU TO DR. HERBERT VON RHINE. DESIGNER OF THE L-15 SPACE SHUTTLE.
SO, MY FRIENDS. WHAT DO YOU THINK OF HER?

SEPTEMBER 12TH.
MBAAHHHHH!!!
WILLIAM, YOU'VE BEEN SULKING LIKE A SPOILT CHILD FOR THE LAST FIFTEEN MINUTES. IF YOU WANT TO TAKE THE CONTROLS, YOU ONLY HAVE TO ASK.
THOROUGHLY DECENT OF YOU OLD BOY, DON'T MIND IF I DO.

VON RHINE SAID NOT TO TAKE IT PAST MACH 3 UNTIL THE AIG UNIT WAS FITTED.
WILLIAM?
WILLIAM!!!!!!

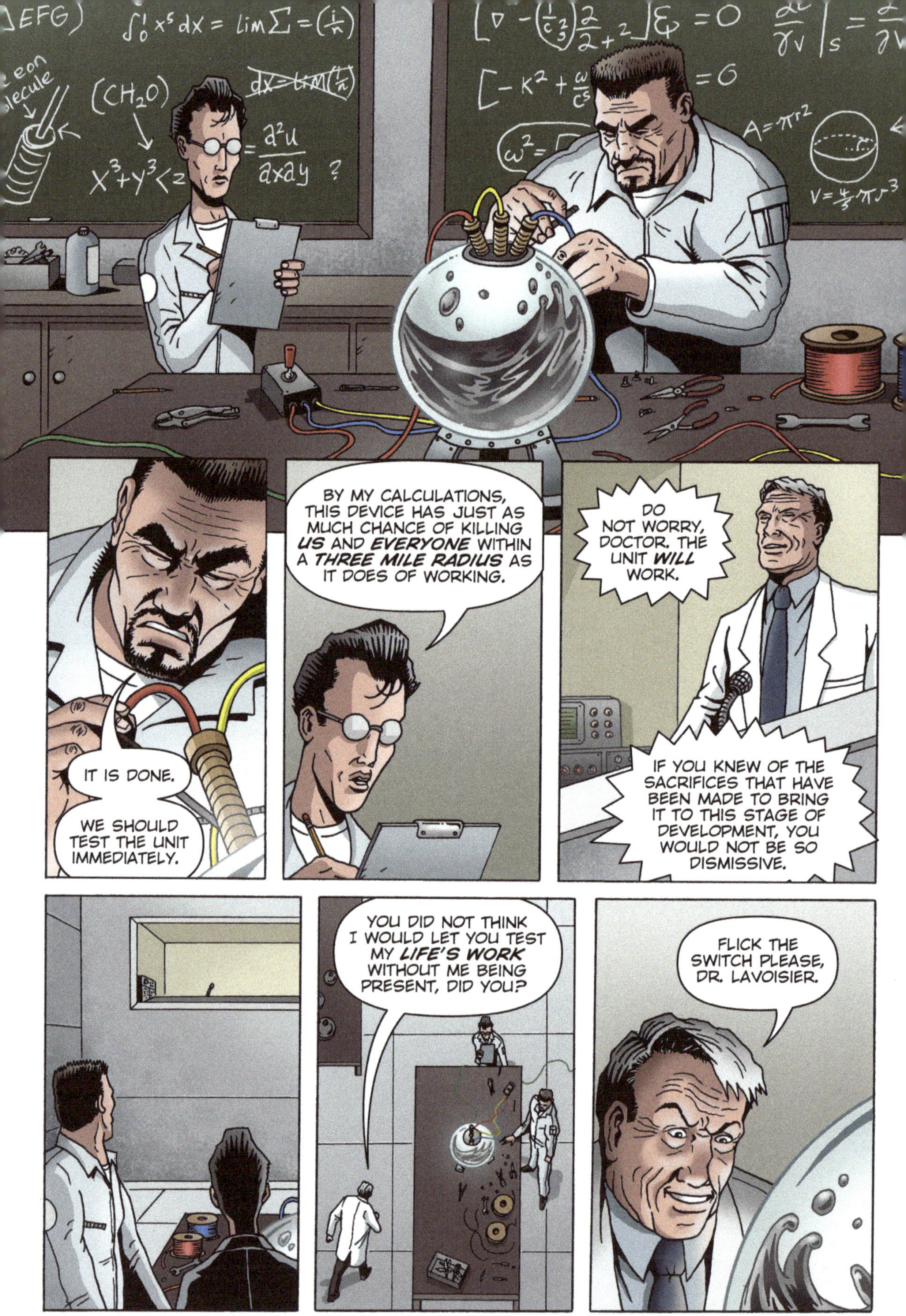

IT IS DONE.

WE SHOULD TEST THE UNIT IMMEDIATELY.

BY MY CALCULATIONS, THIS DEVICE HAS JUST AS MUCH CHANCE OF KILLING ***US*** AND ***EVERYONE*** WITHIN A ***THREE MILE RADIUS*** AS IT DOES OF WORKING.

DO NOT WORRY, DOCTOR. THE UNIT ***WILL*** WORK.

IF YOU KNEW OF THE SACRIFICES THAT HAVE BEEN MADE TO BRING IT TO THIS STAGE OF DEVELOPMENT, YOU WOULD NOT BE SO DISMISSIVE.

CLICK
IT WORKS!
MY ANTI-GRAVITY ENGINE WORKS!
CLICK!
TUNK
THUNK
CLUNK

Switch off that LIGHT!
LESS LIGHT MORE PLANES
BONJOUR.
HOW WAS THE TEST FLIGHT?
NOT BAD JACKY, OLD BOY, NOT BAD.
MY NAME IS *JACQUES*, NOT *JAUCKY*.
OF *COURSE* IT IS OLD BOY, OF *COURSE* IT IS.
WHERE'S OUR RUSSIAN FRIEND?
HE SAYS THAT HE IS WRITING A LETTER TO HIS WIFE.
AND THAT HE DOES NOT CARE FOR YOUR IDEA OF RECREATION.

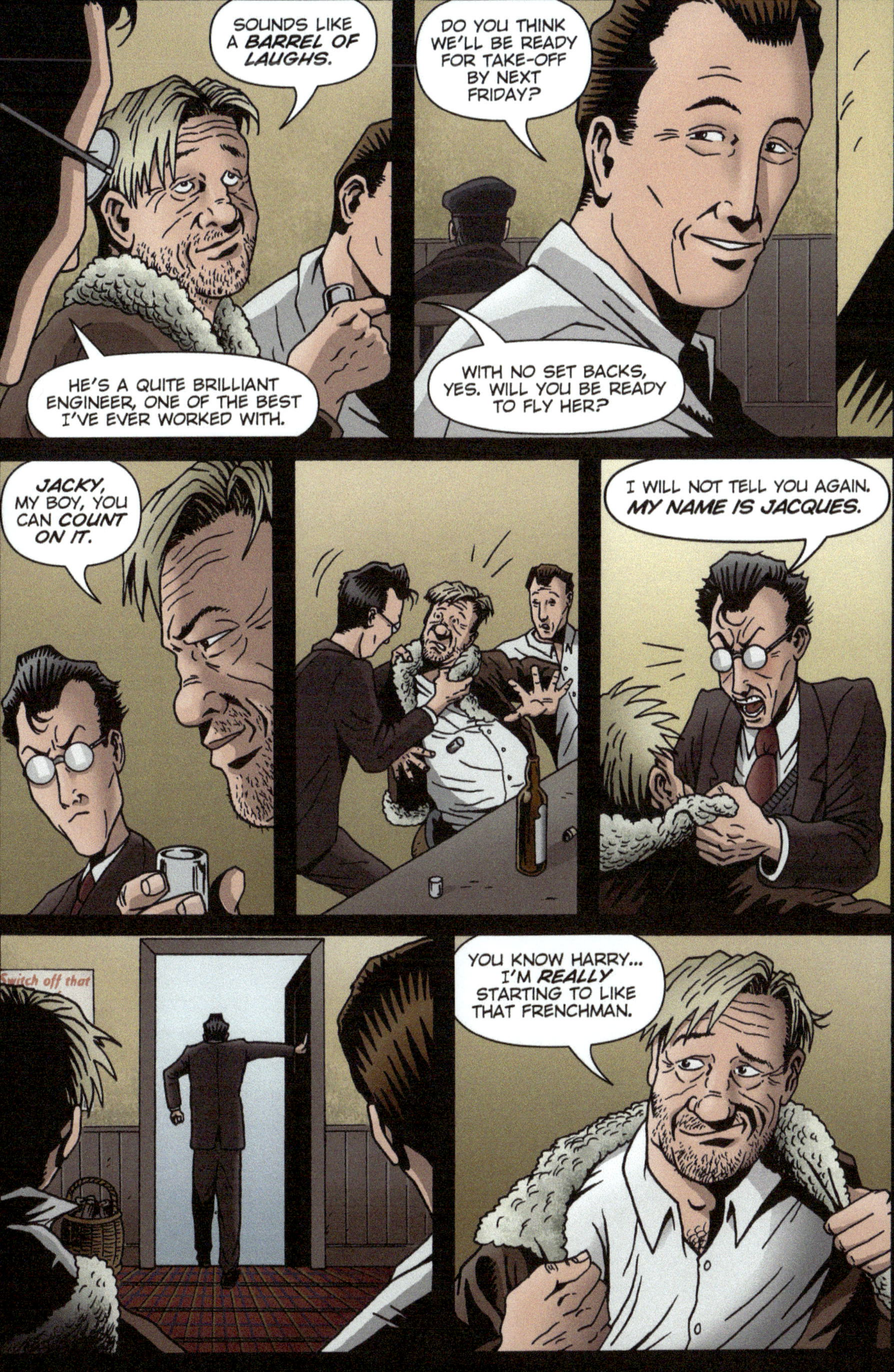

SOUNDS LIKE A ***BARREL OF LAUGHS.***

HE'S A QUITE BRILLIANT ENGINEER, ONE OF THE BEST I'VE EVER WORKED WITH.

DO YOU THINK WE'LL BE READY FOR TAKE-OFF BY NEXT FRIDAY?

WITH NO SET BACKS, YES. WILL YOU BE READY TO FLY HER?

***JACKY,*** MY BOY, YOU CAN ***COUNT ON IT.***

I WILL NOT TELL YOU AGAIN. ***MY NAME IS JACQUES.***

INJECTION SYSTEM
MAINTENANCE HATCH
DEVICE ACTIVATED

never in my life have I... stupid fish and chip eating cretin...
AH, VLADIMIR... I THOUGHT YOU WERE WRITING A LETTER TO YOUR WIFE.
YES, I WAS... I LEFT MY NOTEBOOK IN THE LABORATORY.

My Dearest Irina,
Please forgive me for not writing sooner. I have been extremely busy since arriving here. The mission seems even more difficult than I feared, and is not helped by the antics of my comrades.

The American, although somewhat decadent, is at least committed to the mission and keeps himself in good physical condition. He tells me he is a family man and because of this I am willing to give him the benefit of the doubt.

The Frenchman is stranger. He is undoubtedly brilliant in the field of physics and science but he seems utterly absorbed by himself. There seems to be no trace of modesty in him.

As for the Englishman, I have no idea why he is even here. He is lazy, immoral and very possibly an alcoholic. I shall not miss him when I return home to you.

I have already written to General Melnikov. I am watching them carefully. I have already informed him that the Americans are working with a former Nazi.
How quickly they forget.

I must finish now. There is much to do before we leave for our strange destination.
Know that I am thinking of you, and that I love you,
Vladimir.

LOOK CHAPS, ALL I'M SAYING IS THAT I DON'T SEE THE NEED FOR THIS **BLOODY** ANTI-GRAVITY THINGAMAJIG.
WE ALREADY KNOW IT'S NOT EVEN POWERFUL ENOUGH TO GET US OFF THE GROUND.
I KNOW WHY YOU'RE WORRIED, WILLIAM. IT'S AN UNTRIED PIECE OF EQUIPMENT...
BUT IF VON RHINE SAYS THAT IT WILL HELP US GET OFF THE MOON, THEN PERSONALLY I'M INCLINED TO TAKE MY CHANCES WITH IT.
ALL THE LABORATORY TESTS SO FAR HAVE BEEN SUCCESSFUL...
ITS GRAVITY CANCELING INFLUENCE IS NOT STRONG ENOUGH TO ALLOW THE *L-15* TO ESCAPE THE EARTH'S PULL, BUT IT WILL BE QUITE SUFFICIENT WHEN LEAVING THE LUNAR SURFACE.
WHAT SAY YOU, VLAD OLD BOY?
WITHOUT A VERTICAL TAKE-OFF SYSTEM WE HAVE NO CHOICE BUT TO USE IT. THE SHUTTLE WOULD NOT BE ABLE TAKE OFF FROM THE LUNAR SURFACE WITHOUT IT.
ALTHOUGH, I AGREE THAT THE GERMAN SEEMS PARTICULARLY KEEN ON IT BEING INCORPORATED INTO THE SHUTTLE'S PROPULSION SYSTEM.

OH, I WOULD NOT SAY "KEEN". I MERELY WISH TO GIVE YOU THE GREATEST CHANCE OF RETURNING TO EARTH ALIVE.

I KNOW BETTER THAN MOST WHAT IT IS LIKE TO MISS YOUR HOMELAND. I WOULD HATE TO THINK OF YOU STRANDED UP THERE, ALONE, LOOKING UP AT THE DISTANT EARTH AS YOUR OXYGEN SUPPLY RUNS OUT.

IT IS COMPLETE.
EXCELLENT WORK, PROFESSOR GRUSOV.

THE DAY OF RECKONING DRAWS NEAR.

SEPTEMBER 16TH.
BUT I AM A MAN OF SCIENCE, I HAVE NO NEED FOR AUTOMATIC WEAPONS.
U.S. ARMY
U.S. ARMY
HA! THAT'S WHAT EVERYONE SAYS...
UNTIL THE MERDE HITS THE FAN.
SOME OF YOU WILL ALREADY KNOW THE THOMPSON - HELL OF A WEAPON. THESE HAVE BEEN MODIFIED BY THE SCIENCE BODS. THEY SHOULD WORK IN THE LUNAR ENVIRONMENT.
SHOULD?
PERSONALLY, I JUST HOPE THAT WE DO NOT EXPLODE INTO A MILLION PIECES AS SOON AS THE JET ENGINES IGNITE.
I'LL SECOND THAT.
COMPOSITION B+
COMPOSITION B+
AND IF THE GUNS AND EXPLOSIVES DON'T WORK... IT'S ALWAYS ADVISABLE TO HAVE A BACK UP PLAN!
...WHAT!!!

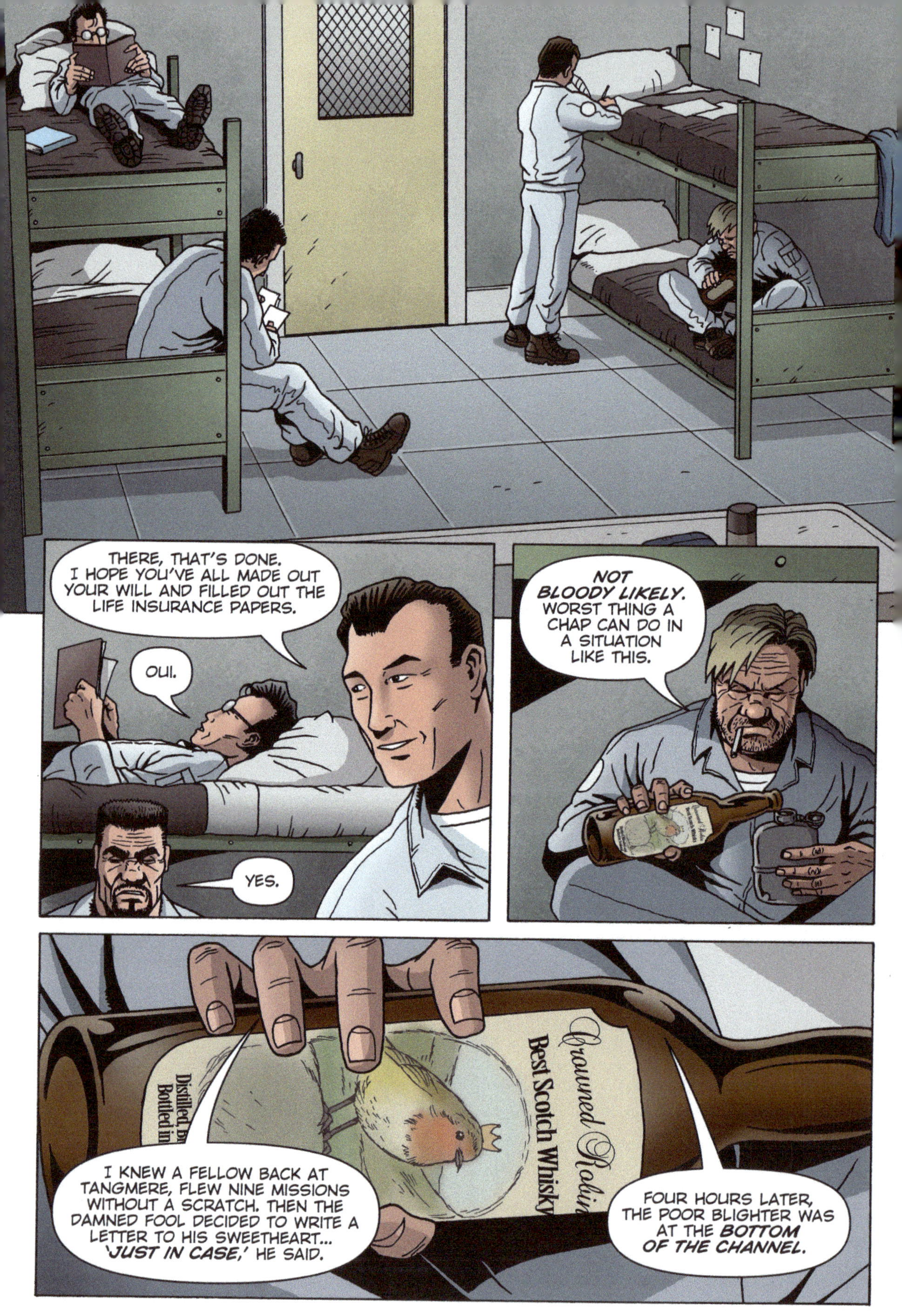

THERE, THAT'S DONE. I HOPE YOU'VE ALL MADE OUT YOUR WILL AND FILLED OUT THE LIFE INSURANCE PAPERS.

OUI.

YES.

***NOT BLOODY LIKELY.*** WORST THING A CHAP CAN DO IN A SITUATION LIKE THIS.

FRIDAY, SEPTEMBER 19TH, 1947.
1.24 AM.
LAUNCH NIGHT.
BEGINNING COUNTDOWN. GOOD LUCK GENTLEMEN.
BEST OF LUCK, MY FRIENDS...
WE'LL SEE YOU IN A WEEK.
TEN... NINE...

EIGHT...
SEVEN...
SIX...
HOLD ON TO YOUR HATS, BOYS.
FIVE...
FOUR...
THREE...
TWO...
ONE...
PER ARDUA AD ASTRA!!!

LIFT
OFF

THAT'S FIVE MINUTES SINCE TAKE OFF, GENTLEMEN.
BOOSTER ROCKETS JETTISONED.
YOU'RE LOOKING *BEAUTIFUL!*
YOU'RE *TOO* KIND, OLD BOY. *TOO BLOODY KIND.*
RELEASING CLAMPS.
RELEASE CLAMPS
FUEL TANK AWAY.
SHUTTLE ENGINE ENGAGED.

T-PLUS 46 HOURS, 27 MINUTES:
OXYGEN SUPPLY IS HOLDING STEADY, SIR. WE HAD A BRIEF SPIKE IN PRESSURE BUT WE WERE ABLE TO RECTIFY IT WITHOUT NOTIFYING THE CREW.
GOOD WORK. THEY'VE GOT ENOUGH ON THEIR PLATES AS IT IS.
WHAT ABOUT THIS ANTI-GRAVITY DEVICE... EVERYTHING OKAY WITH THAT?
I SHOULD HOPE SO, HERR SPEARS. IF IT MALFUNCTIONS IT WILL NOT BE POSSIBLE FOR THEM TO LAND SAFELY.
...OR TO EVER LEAVE THE LUNAR SURFACE.
YOU'RE A REAL OPTIMIST, AREN'T YOU VON RHINE.
I WAS MERELY POSTULATING THE SCENARI--
APPROACHING THE LUNAR SURFACE, GENTLEMEN.

PREPARING TO DISENGAGE AUTOPILOT.
DOES THAT MEAN I HAVE TO PUT THAT BALLY GOLDFISH BOWL BACK ON MY HEAD?
NINETY SECONDS FROM THE SURFACE.
COPY THAT, HARRY... MAINTAIN PRESENT COURSE.
NO ONE WARNED US ABOUT THE BLOODY STINK ONCE WE PUT THOSE HELMETS ON. REEKS OF WHISKEY AND NAVY CUT!
I THINK THAT IS JUST YOURS.
HA! YOU MIGHT BE RIGHT, VLAD OLD BOY...
YOU MIGHT BE RIGHT!
TWO HUNDRED FEET FROM LUNAR SURFACE... I'M ABOUT TO ENGAGE THE A/G UNIT.
ANTI-GRAVITY UNIT ENGAGED.
DETONATION IMMINENT
WELL CHAPS... THAT SEEMED TO GO OFF WITHOUT A HITCH...

JESUS BLOODY WEPT! WHAT THE HELL WAS THAT?!
THE A/G UNIT IS OFF LINE! THE ENGINES... THE FUEL INJECTORS... THE ENTIRE PROPULSION SYSTEM IS GONE!
WHAT DO YOU MEAN, HOW CAN IT BE GONE?

WHAT THE HELL JUST HAPPENED?
WHY HAVEN'T I GOT A GODDAMN RADIO FEED?
RADIO IS DEAD. PROPULSION MONITORS ARE OFF LINE. EVERYTHING IS... IM NOT GETTING A SIGNAL.

WHAT ABOUT LIFE SUPPORT?
GONE TOO... IT'S LIKE THEY JUST VANISHED.

GET JACKINGTON DOWN HERE, NOW!
I - I MUST GO TO MY OFFICE. THERE IS A LOT OF NEW DATA TO SORT THROUGH.

GUHHHHHHHHHHHHHMMM
YESSSS... THE EXPLOSSSION WILL HAVE KILLED THEM ALL... THEY COULD NOT HAVE SSURVIVED THE BLASSST.
...OUR PLAN IS SSSTILL IN PLACE.

OKAY, WILLIAM, LET'S GET THE SHUTTLE POWERED DOWN BEFORE SOMETHING ELSE EXPLODES. VLADIMIR, GO DOWN TO THE CARGO BAY, GATHER AS MUCH GEAR AS YOU CAN SALVAGE AND PACK IT INTO THE LEEP.

JACQUES, SEE IF YOU CAN FIGURE OUT WHAT HAPPENED. AND CHECK THAT THE PORTABLE TRANSMITTER IS STILL FUNCTIONING.

I'LL GO OUTSIDE AND CHECK OUT THE DAMAGE. DON'T FORGET TO ACTIVATE THE GRAVITY INDUCERS ON YOUR SUITS BEFORE YOU LEAVE THE SHUTTLE.

*SON OF A - -*

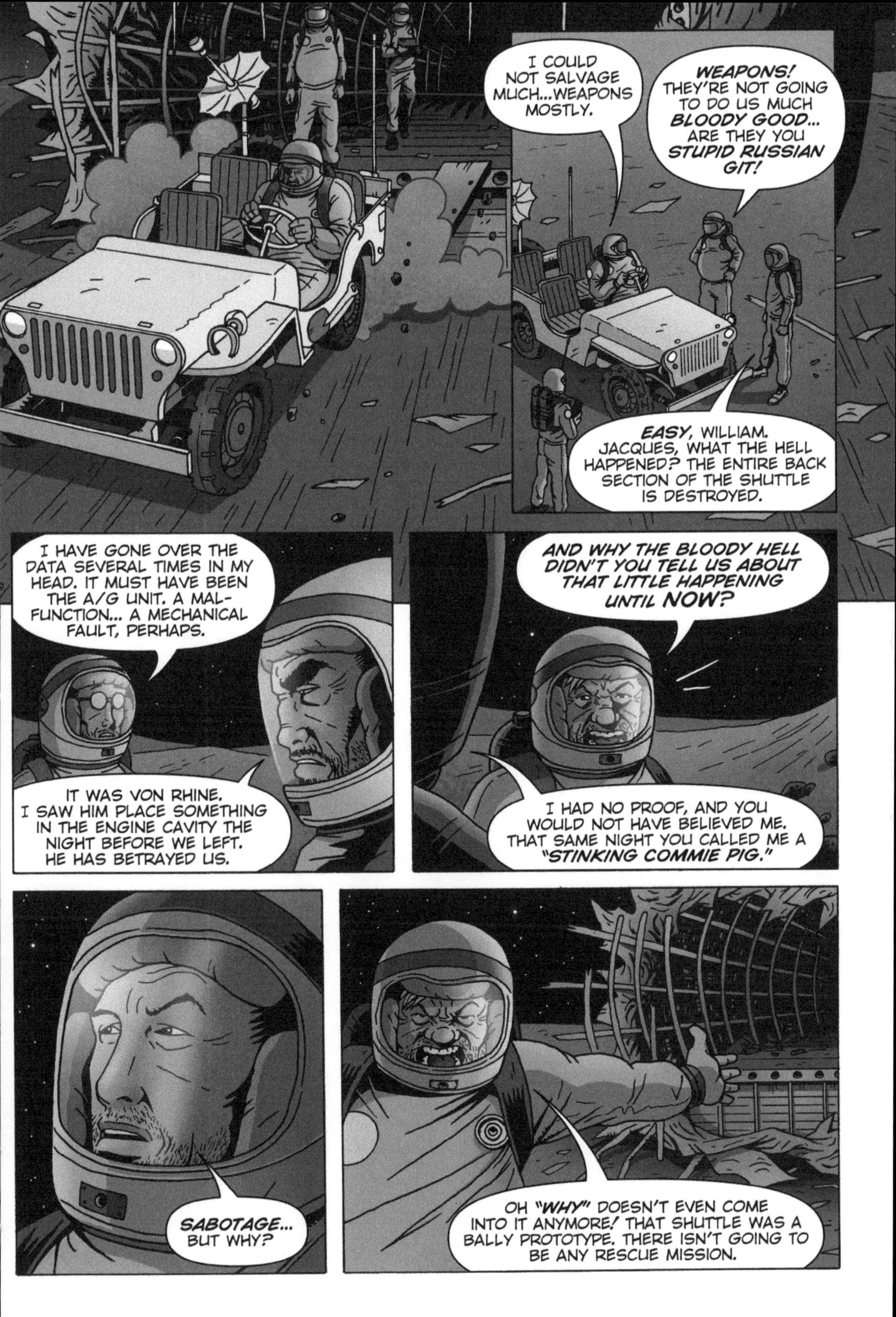

I COULD NOT SALVAGE MUCH...WEAPONS MOSTLY.

*WEAPONS!* THEY'RE NOT GOING TO DO US MUCH *BLOODY GOOD...* ARE THEY YOU *STUPID RUSSIAN GIT!*

*EASY,* WILLIAM. JACQUES, WHAT THE HELL HAPPENED? THE ENTIRE BACK SECTION OF THE SHUTTLE IS DESTROYED.

I HAVE GONE OVER THE DATA SEVERAL TIMES IN MY HEAD. IT MUST HAVE BEEN THE A/G UNIT. A MAL-FUNCTION... A MECHANICAL FAULT, PERHAPS.

IT WAS VON RHINE. I SAW HIM PLACE SOMETHING IN THE ENGINE CAVITY THE NIGHT BEFORE WE LEFT. HE HAS BETRAYED US.

*AND WHY THE BLOODY HELL DIDN'T YOU TELL US ABOUT THAT LITTLE HAPPENING UNTIL NOW?*

I HAD NO PROOF, AND YOU WOULD NOT HAVE BELIEVED ME. THAT SAME NIGHT YOU CALLED ME A *"STINKING COMMIE PIG."*

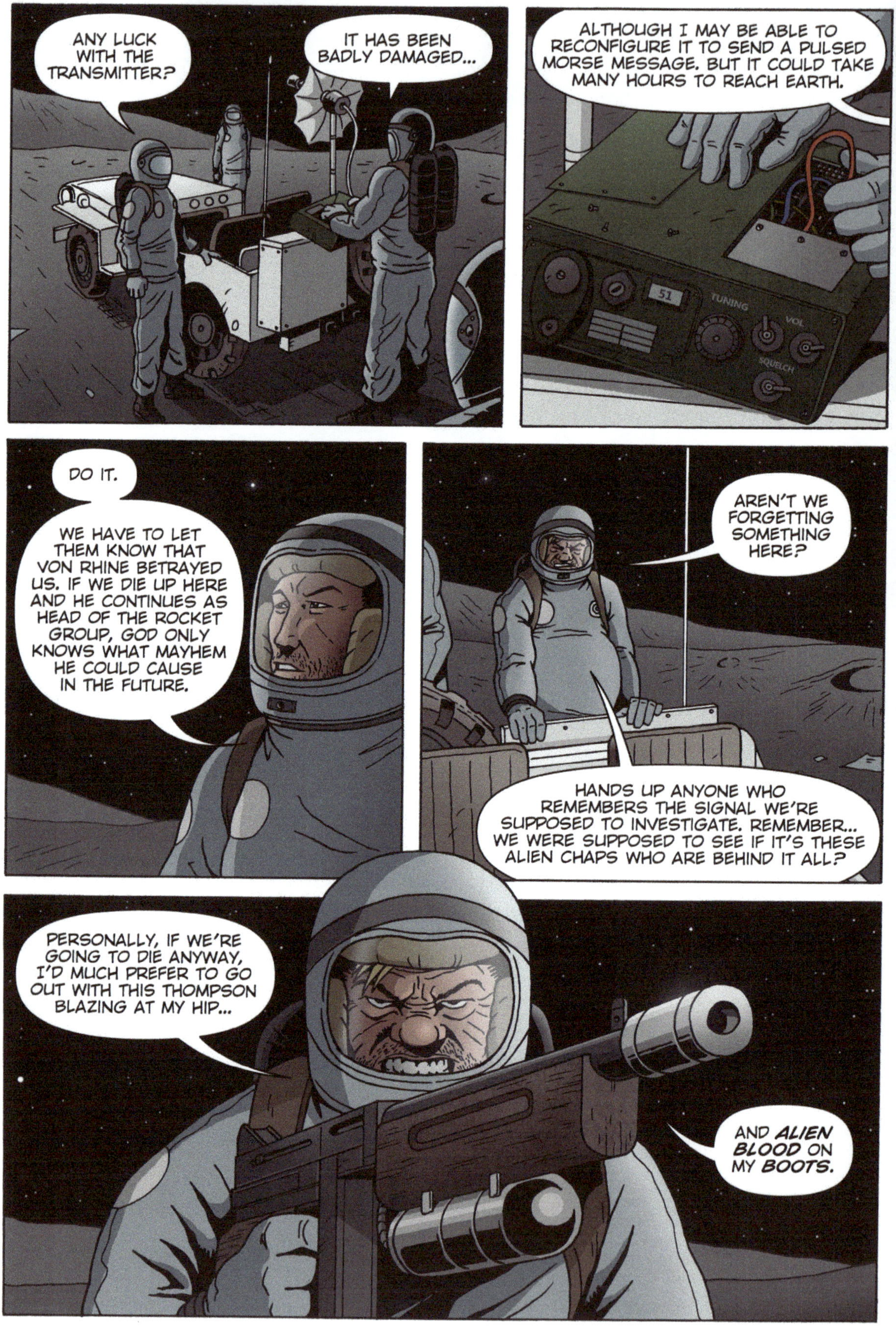

DO IT.

WE HAVE TO LET THEM KNOW THAT VON RHINE BETRAYED US. IF WE DIE UP HERE AND HE CONTINUES AS HEAD OF THE ROCKET GROUP, GOD ONLY KNOWS WHAT MAYHEM HE COULD CAUSE IN THE FUTURE.

AREN'T WE FORGETTING SOMETHING HERE?

HANDS UP ANYONE WHO REMEMBERS THE SIGNAL WE'RE SUPPOSED TO INVESTIGATE. REMEMBER... WE WERE SUPPOSED TO SEE IF IT'S THESE ALIEN CHAPS WHO ARE BEHIND IT ALL?

PERSONALLY, IF WE'RE GOING TO DIE ANYWAY, I'D MUCH PREFER TO GO OUT WITH THIS THOMPSON BLAZING AT MY HIP...

AND ***ALIEN BLOOD*** ON MY ***BOOTS***.

HOW LONG SINCE WE LOST CONTACT?
FORTY TWO MINUTES, SIR.
AND HOW LONG WILL THE OXYGEN SUPPLY IN THEIR SUITS LAST?
FULLY TANKED, FOUR HOURS, BUT... WE DON'T EVEN KNOW IF THEY--
I DON'T WANT TO HEAR IT! UNTIL WE KNOW FOR CERTAIN... WE PRESUME THAT THEY'RE *ALIVE*.
HAVE THEY ANY OTHER MEANS OF CONTACTING US?
ALONG WITH THE MAIN COMMUNICATION SYSTEM THEY ALSO HAVE A BACK UP TRANSMITTER, BUT IF THEY WERE USING THAT WE WOULD HAVE HEARD FROM THEM BY NOW.
JUST MAKE SURE YOU KEEP ALL THE CHANNELS OPEN.
GODDAMNIT. THERE'S STILL A CHANCE.

SO IT'S AGREED? WE CHECK OUT THE SIGNAL.

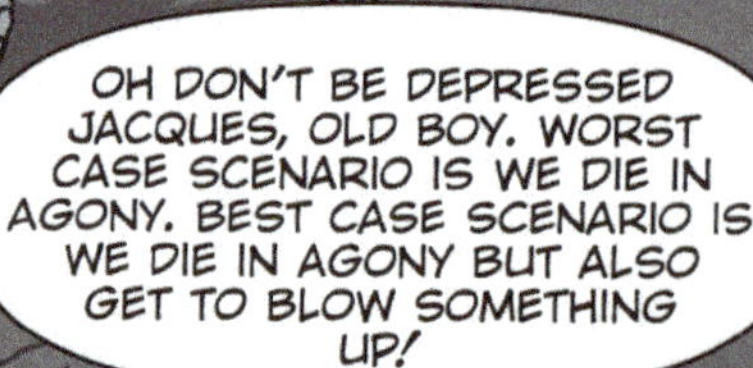
OUI. IT SEEMS WE ARE TO DIE EITHER WAY. WE SHOULD TRY TO DO SOME GOOD BEFORE WE EXPIRE. FOR OUR COUNTRYMEN, AND FOR SCIENCE.
OH DON'T BE DEPRESSED JACQUES, OLD BOY. WORST CASE SCENARIO IS WE DIE IN AGONY. BEST CASE SCENARIO IS WE DIE IN AGONY BUT ALSO GET TO BLOW SOMETHING UP!

MONSIEUR BROWN, YOU CALLED ME "JACQUES."

YES, OLD BEAN, IT RATHER SEEMS I DID.
LOOK, I'M SORRY IF I'VE BEEN A BIT OF A PILL BUT, WELL, I'D JUST LIKE TO SAY THAT... I CAN'T THINK OF THREE CHAPS I'D RATHER BE FACING CERTAIN DEATH WITH.

WELL SAID, WILLIAM.
WE'RE DONE FOR EITHER WAY. IF IT'S ALIENS BEHIND THIS SIGNAL WE CAN AT LEAST TRY TO GET A WARNING TO EARTH WITH THE TRANSMITTER. HELL, WE MIGHT EVEN TAKE A FEW OF THEM WITH US.

AGREED?

AGREED.

AGREED.

OUI.

THE SIGNAL IS COMING FROM A LARGE CRATER THREE MILES TO THE EAST.
WHEN WE GET TO THE TOP... KEEP LOW.
GOD ONLY KNOWS WHAT WE'RE GOING TO SEE DOWN THERE.

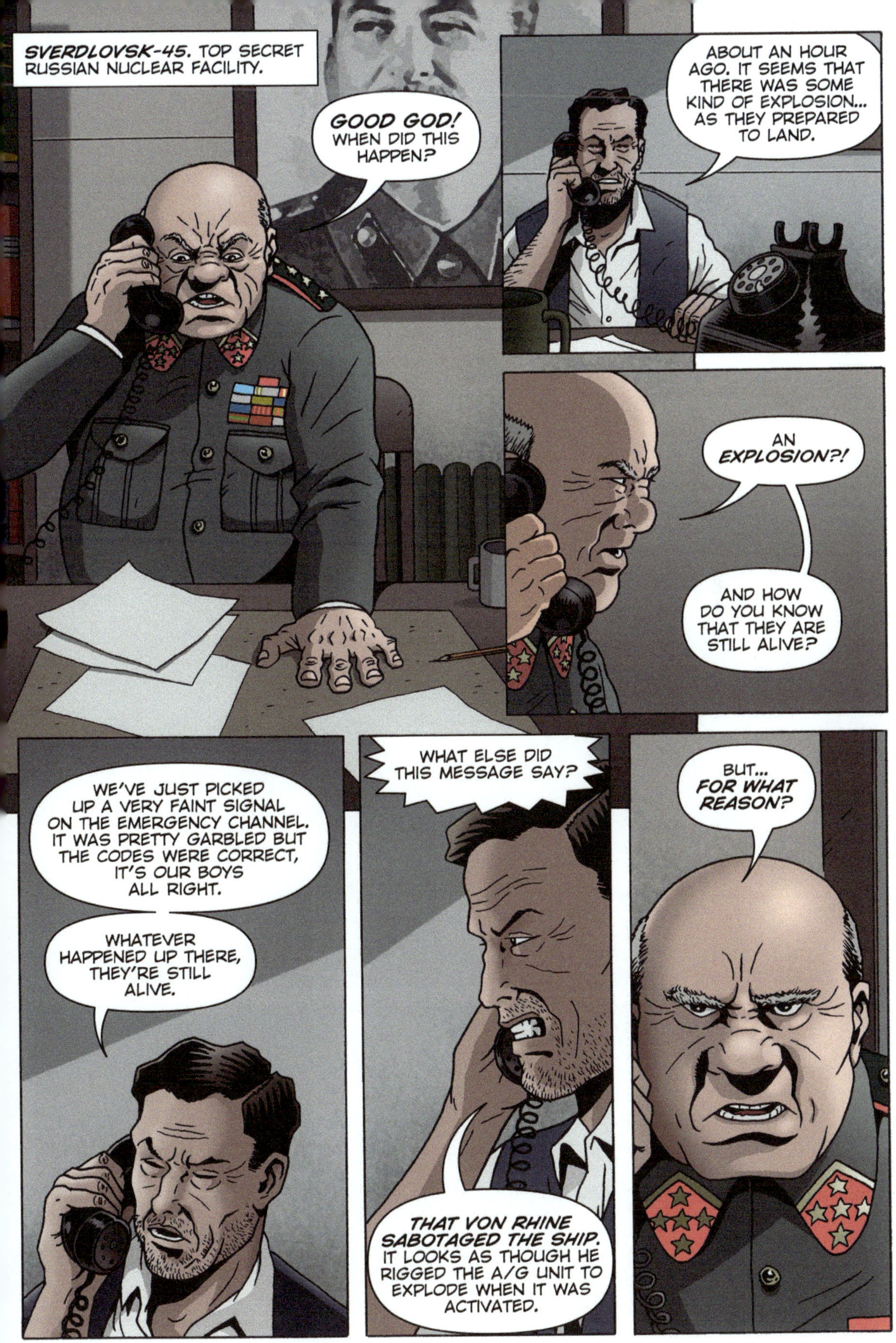

*SVERDLOVSK-45.* TOP SECRET RUSSIAN NUCLEAR FACILITY.

*GOOD GOD!* WHEN DID THIS HAPPEN?

ABOUT AN HOUR AGO. IT SEEMS THAT THERE WAS SOME KIND OF EXPLOSION... AS THEY PREPARED TO LAND.

AN *EXPLOSION?!*

AND HOW DO YOU KNOW THAT THEY ARE STILL ALIVE?

TALLY HO, BOYS! LET'S GIVE THE BLIGHTERS BLOODY HELL!!

GOD KNOWS. I KNEW WE WERE WRONG TO TRUST A BLOODY NAZI. HE'S GONE MISSING. NO ONE HAS SEEN HIM SINCE WE LOST CONTACT WITH THE CREW.
I HAVE TO GO NOW, GENERAL MELNIKOV.
YES, YES, I UNDERSTAND.
PLEASE KEEP ME INFORMED OF ANY FURTHER DEVELOPMENTS.
GET COMMISSAR BULGANIN ON THE PHONE. I'VE JUST HEARD THE MOST TERRIBLE NEWS.
GUHHHHHHHHHHHMMM
LETVINSKY, WAKE UP MAN! WHAT THE HELL DO YOU THINK YOU ARE DOING?
GUHHHHHH
I-I-I'M SORRY, SIR. I... I HAVE NOT BEEN FEELING WELL.
I-I ASSURE YOU... IT WILL NOT HAPPEN AGAIN.

BUDDA
BUDDA
BUDDA
BUDDA DDA BUD BUDDA BUDDA
BUDDA
BUDDA
WE DON'T HAVE MUCH TIME!
JACQUES, VLADIMIR, YOU TWO TRY AND INFILTRATE THAT COMMAND BUILDING. TRY TO FIND OUT WHAT THE HELL IS GOING ON HERE.
WILLIAM, WE'RE GOING TO TRY TO GET ONE OF THOSE GODDAMN SAUCERS INTO THE AIR.

HUUNHHHH!
UDDA BUDDA BUDDA BUDD

DON'T SHOOT!
PLEASE! DON'T SHOOT!
YES, DON'T SHOOT...
WE COME IN PEACE!
SKRUTCH
SHLOOP

THANKS WILLIAM, THAT WAS CLOSE.
YES, THESE ALIEN CHAPS SEEM TO BE EVERYWHERE. WE REALLY SHOULD KEEP AN *EYE OUT* FOR THEM!
HA HA HA!!
BUDDA BUDDA

BUDDA
BUDDA
ZATT
WHERE DO WE GO?
JUST PICK A DOOR!
BUDDA
BUDDA
COME, WE MUST FIND COVER.
ZATT
ZATT
ZATT
IT LOOKS LIKE SOME KIND OF LABORATORY.

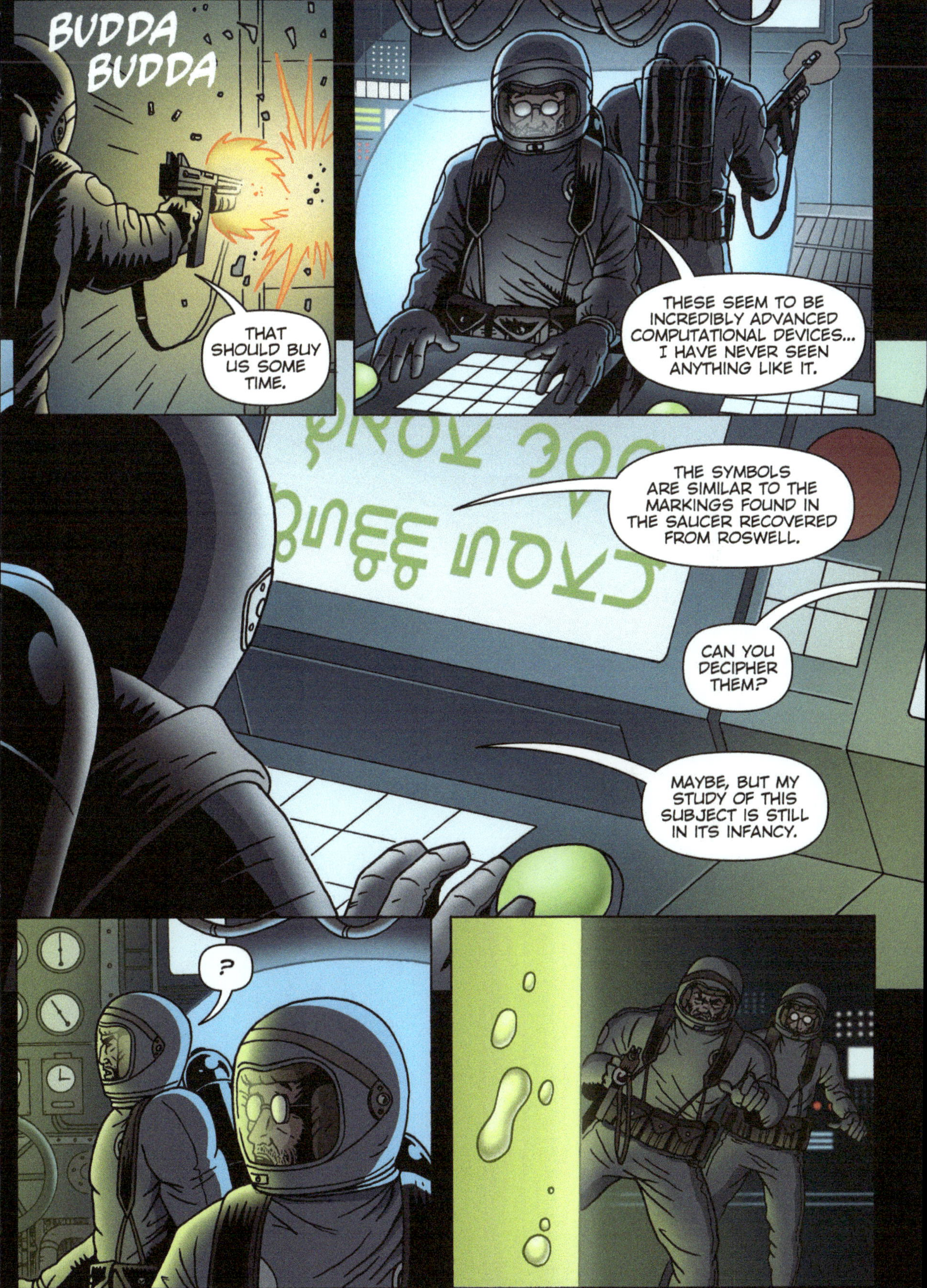
BUDDA BUDDA
THAT SHOULD BUY US SOME TIME.
THESE SEEM TO BE INCREDIBLY ADVANCED COMPUTATIONAL DEVICES... I HAVE NEVER SEEN ANYTHING LIKE IT.
THE SYMBOLS ARE SIMILAR TO THE MARKINGS FOUND IN THE SAUCER RECOVERED FROM ROSWELL.
CAN YOU DECIPHER THEM?
MAYBE, BUT MY STUDY OF THIS SUBJECT IS STILL IN ITS INFANCY.
?

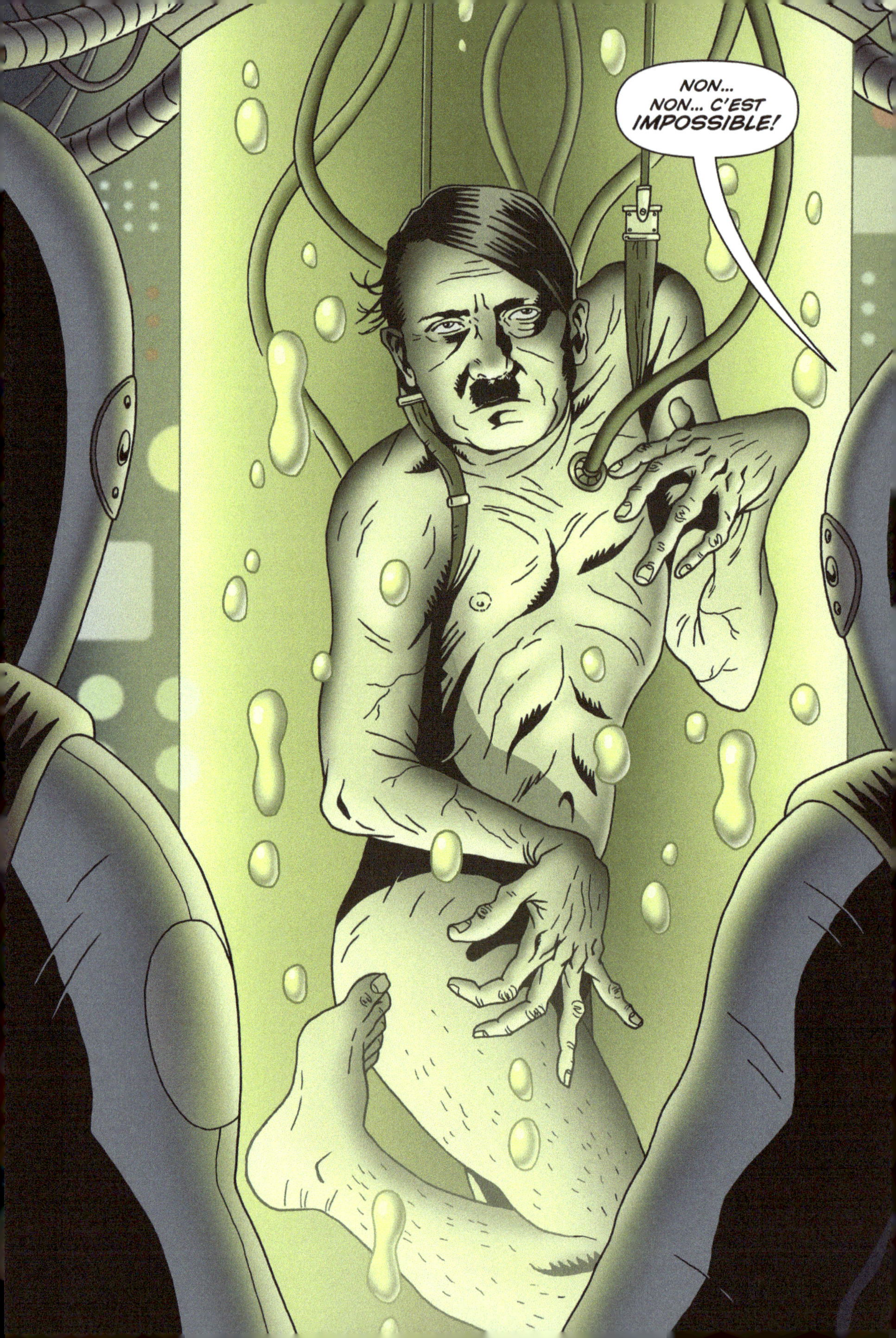
NON... NON... C'EST IMPOSSIBLE!

I'LL SEE THAT BASTARD *HANG* FOR THIS!
HOW LONG HAS HE BEEN IN THERE?
HE LOCKED HIMSELF IN ABOUT TEN MINUTES AGO, SIR.
WE DIDN'T WANT TO USE FORCE WITHOUT YOUR SAY SO.
CRACKKKK!
GUUNNNNNNNNNNHHH
*WHAT IN GOD'S NAME?*

...IT APPEARS TO BE AN ABANDONED CLONING PROGRAMME.
ABANDONED? BUT WHY?
THEY DO NOT SEEM TO HAVE BEEN ABLE TO PERFECT THE TISSUE REPRODUCTION. THERE WERE PROBLEMS, GENETIC ABNORMALITIES, SEVERE DEFORMATIONS OF THE MUSCULATURE AND THE SKELETON.
DID YOU HEAR THAT?
A SOUND... FROM BEHIND THAT DOOR.
READY?
OUI.
BUDDA
BUDDA

BUDDA
BUDDA
BUDDA

COME ON, HARRY... ROTTEN EGG AND ALL THAT!
ZATT
ZATT
WE'VE GOT TO GET THIS THING INTO THE SKY.
THIS IS A FULL BLOWN *INVASION FLEET!*
LOOK WHAT I PICKED UP! SHOULD FETCH A PRETTY PENNY IF WE EVER MAKE IT BACK TO EARTH.
LOOK HARRY, WE'VE GOT VISITORS!

THAT'S IT HARRY... BY JOVE, YOU'VE GOT THE MEASURE OF HER!
HMM... I WONDER WHAT THIS BUTTON DOES?
CLICK
BZZZT
BZAAK
DAMN GOOD SHOOTING, WILLIAM!
GIVE 'EM HELL!!!
BZAAK
CERTAINLY WILL, OLD BEAN...
CERTAINLY WILL!
BZAAK

WHY DID YOU SABOTAGE THE MISSION?
WHAT THE HELL IS GOING ON?

FOOLISSSH EARTHLING... WE HAVE BEEN IN CONTROL ALL ALONG...
YOUR PRECIOUSSSS PLANET... IS OURSSSSSSS...

GOOD GOD! HE'S... HE'S BEING CONTROLLED!
THE ALIENS! THEY'RE CONTROLLING HIS MIND!!

SSSIMPLE CREATURESSS... SSO TRUSSSTING.

GAAAUGGGHH!!!
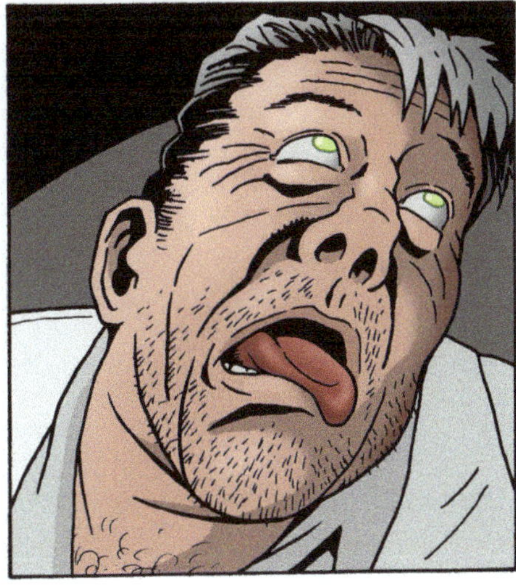

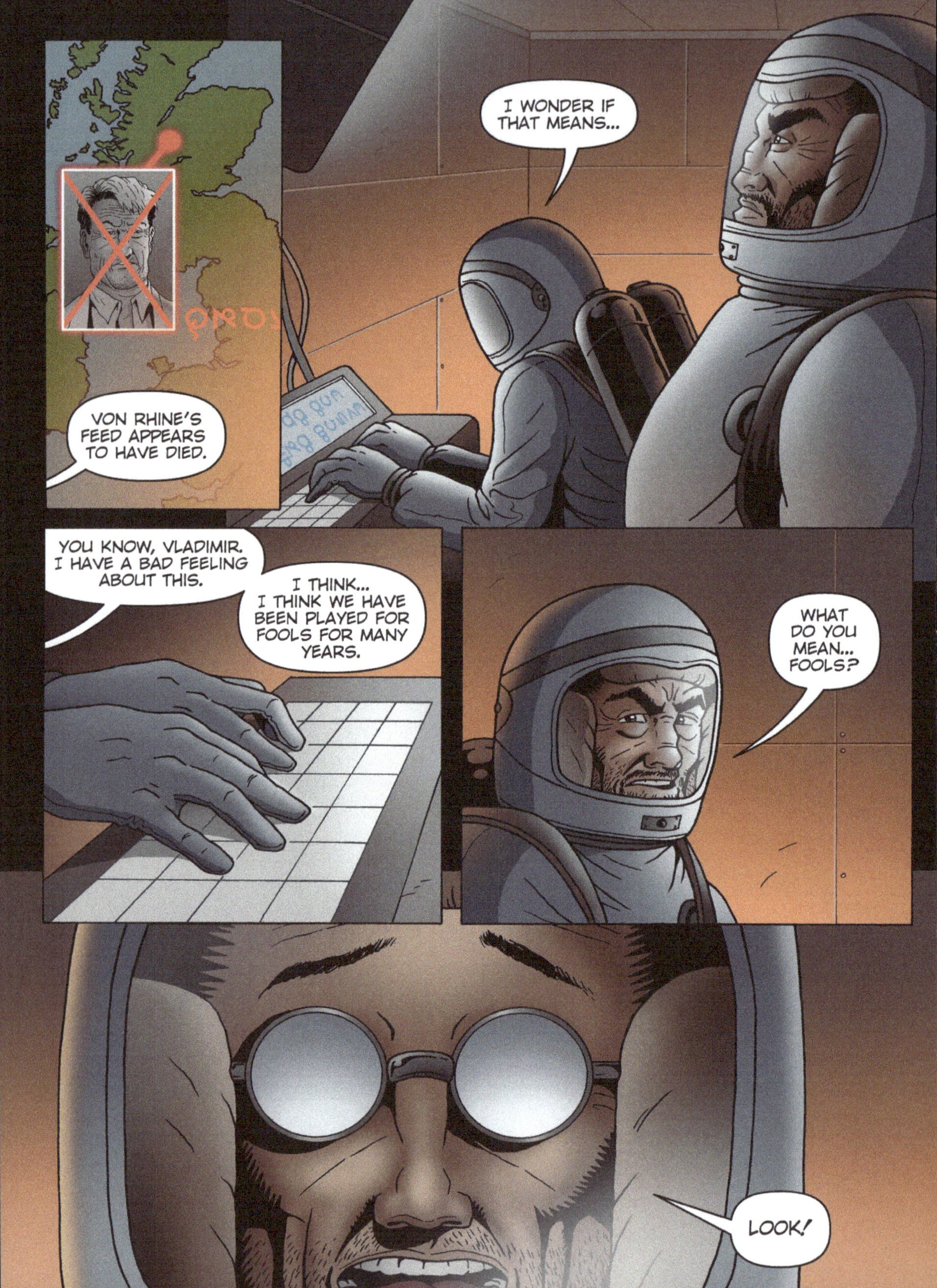
VON RHINE'S FEED APPEARS TO HAVE DIED.
I WONDER IF THAT MEANS...
YOU KNOW, VLADIMIR. I HAVE A BAD FEELING ABOUT THIS.
I THINK... I THINK WE HAVE BEEN PLAYED FOR FOOLS FOR MANY YEARS.
WHAT DO YOU MEAN... FOOLS?
LOOK!

HITLER...

MUSSOLINI...

HIROHITO... ALL UNDER *ALIEN CONTROL!*

BUT FOR WHAT PURPOSE?
DON'T YOU SEE VLADIMIR? IT'S SO SIMPLE WHEN YOU THINK ABOUT IT... WHY BOTHER KILLING THE HUMAN RACE YOURSELF, WHEN YOU CAN GET THEM TO KILL EACH OTHER INSTEAD?
WHEN THEIR PLAN FAILED, WHEN THE ALLIES WON THE WAR, I SUPPOSE THAT'S WHEN THEY HAD TO START PLANNING THEIR INVASION.

HELLO.
YES, GENERAL MELNIKOV! PLEASE LISTEN MAN, WHAT I'M ABOUT TO TELL YOU IS GOING TO SOUND INSANE, BUT... YOU MUST BELIEVE ME.
WE'RE SURE THAT VON RHINE WAS BEING CONTROLLED BY THESE ALIEN TYPES. THEY SEEM TO HAVE BEEN ABLE TO TAP DIRECTLY INTO HIS BRAIN.
GOD KNOWS HOW MANY PEOPLE THEY'VE CORRUPTED THIS WAY. THEY LOOK ENTIRELY NORMAL...
BUT WHEN THEY ARE IN COMMUNICATION WITH THE ENEMY, THEY GO INTO A SORT OF TRANCE STATE.
TRANCE STATE?
HELLO... HELLO...

YES, HE'S A SPY, I TELL YOU! AN ALIEN AGENT! HE'S BEING CONTROLLED BY THE ENEMY!
SHOOT ON SIGHT! I REPEAT, SHOOT ON SIGHT!
YES SIR, HE WAS SEEN FIVE MINUTES AGO, ENTERING THE LAUNCH TUBES. WE'RE ALMOST THERE!
HE'S DISABLED THE ACCESS PANEL, SIR! WE CAN'T GET IN!
THE ALIENS... THEY'RE TRYING TO LAUNCH THE R-1! THEY'LL START ANOTHER WAR!

YESSSS...
YESSS...
ALMOSSSST
DONE...

THESE BEINGS WISH TO TAKE OUR PLANET AS THEIR OWN. THEY WILL EITHER KILL EVERYBODY WE HAVE EVER LOVED... OR ENSLAVE THEM FOREVER.
THE CHOICE IS SIMPLE THEN?
OUI.
BUDDA BUDDA BUDDA
WHAT?
WHAT HAPPENED?

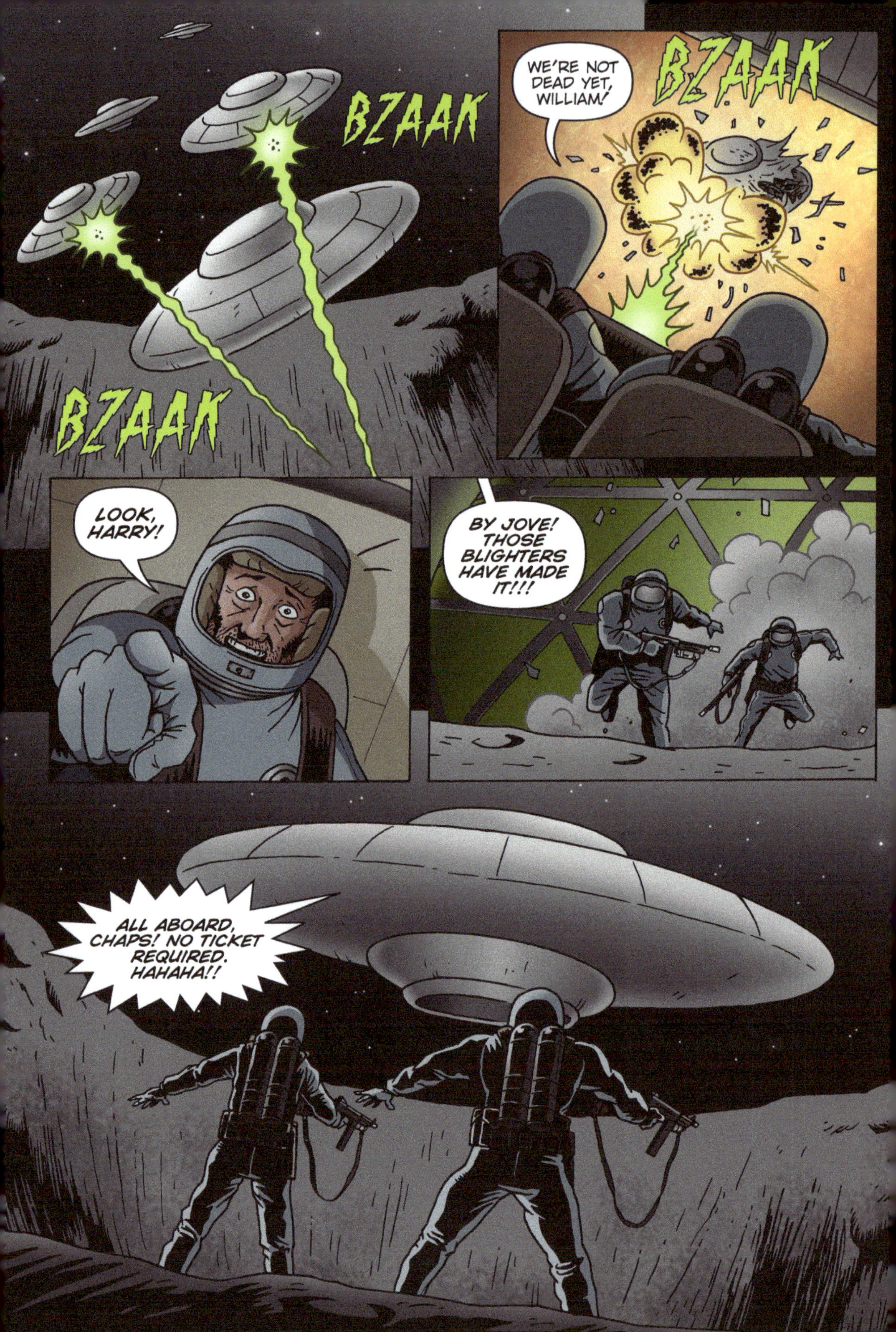
BZAAK
BZAAK
WE'RE NOT DEAD YET, WILLIAM!
BZAAK
LOOK, HARRY!
BY JOVE! THOSE BLIGHTERS HAVE MADE IT!!!
ALL ABOARD, CHAPS! NO TICKET REQUIRED. HAHAHA!!

BZAAK
CRIKEY!!
THANK GOD YOU'RE ALL RIGHT!
BANDITS AT EIGHT O'CLOCK, HARRY!
SWING US ROUND AND I'LL GIVE THEM A BLOODY NOSE!
BZAAK
BOOM

THIS IS IT, MEN.
THERE'S NO GUARANTEE THAT THIS HEAP OF JUNK WILL GET US BACK TO EARTH, BUT AT LEAST WE CAN MAKE SURE THESE ALIEN SLIMEBALLS DON'T GET THERE EITHER.
THE THINGS WE FOUND INSIDE... THE PLOTS THAT WERE REVEALED...
DESTROY IT. LEAVE NOTHING BUT *DUST*.
*NOTHING BUT DUST!*
BZAAK
BZAAK
BZAAK

BZAAK
BZAAK
BZAAK
BOOM
BOOM
I SAY, CHAPS - IF WE DO MAKE IT HOME, I'M GOING TO DRINK A LOT OF WHISKEY.

TWO YEARS LATER.

TWO YEARS OF INNOVATION AND INDUSTRY THE LIKES OF WHICH THIS WORLD HAS NEVER SEEN.

ENEMIES HAVE BECOME ALLIES IN A FIGHT TO SAVE THE WORLD.

LAVOISIER AND GRUSOV HAVE BEEN ABLE TO REVERSE ENGINEER THE ALIEN PISTOL BROUGHT HOME BY BROWN. THE MECHANISMS HAVE BEEN SCRUTINISED, EXPLORED, IMPROVED UPON.

LASER CANNONS LINE THE STREETS AND SQUARES OF EVERY LARGE TOWN AND CITY. FLEETS OF FIGHTER SHUTTLES LIE IN WAIT.

THE COMPUTATIONAL DRIVES OF THE ALIEN CRAFT HELD MANY SECRETS. PLOTS HAVE BEEN REVEALED. TRAITORS HAVE BEEN DEALT WITH. WHEN THE CLONING PROGRAMME FAILED THE ALIENS TRIED THEIR BACK-UP PLAN: MIND CONTROL ON THEIR CHOSEN TARGETS.

IT WAS EFFECTIVE BUT FAR FROM IDEAL, PLACING TOO MUCH STRESS ON THE SYNAPTIC CONNECTIONS OF THE SUBJECTS' BRAINS. HENCE HITLER'S OBVIOUS MENTAL DECLINE THROUGHOUT *1945*.

THE INVADERS WILL RETURN, OF THAT WE CAN BE SURE, AND THE PEOPLE OF EARTH WILL BE READY FOR THEM. THEY WILL COME TO REALISE THAT THE MOST DANGEROUS THING IN THIS INFINITE UNIVERSE IS A HUMAN BEING WITH ITS BACK TO A WALL.

SO, EVERYTHING IS GOING TO PLAN?

YES, SIR BASIL, NO HITCHES SO FAR.
LESS THAN ONE HOUR TO CONTACT, SIR.

SPLENDID! YOU KNOW, IT'S STILL HARD TO BELIEVE THAT THE AXIS POWERS WERE HIJAKED IN 1943. OUR STRANGE VISITORS MUST HAVE BEEN VERY HAPPY TO FIND SUCH AN EVIL MOB ALREADY HARD AT WORK... SO MANY LIVES LOST...
BUT THESE ALIEN CHAPS SEEM TO BE CUT FROM THE SAME CLOTH AS THE NAZIS... NOTHING THEY FEAR MORE THAN A FAIR FIGHT!

YOUR TEA, SIR.
AH, SAMANTHA. THANK YOU, MY DEAR.
I DON'T KNOW WHAT I'D DO WITHOUT YOU.

GOOD LUCK, GENTLEMEN.
I KNOW THAT YOU WON'T LET US DOWN.

WE'LL DO OUR VERY BEST, SIR.
YOU CAN COUNT ON THAT.

OKAY MEN, LET'S JUST STICK TO THE PLAN AND WE'LL ALL BE GOING HOME TONIGHT.
BZAAK
BZAAK
EAT MY SEARING PLASMA BLAST, YOU FILTHY ALIEN BRIGANDS!

DON'T YOU WORRY, MY DEAR.
I'VE GOT A FEELING THAT EVERYTHING IS GOING TO BE ALL RIGHT.
THE END
JIM BOSWELL 2012

# Project Luna
# Bonus Material

PAGE TWENTY-SEVEN
Four panels

PANEL 1
A large panel. Jackington has just shown the men into the main rocket room. It's an enormous hollow cave, two hundred feet high - a James Bond villain's wet dream. The roof is made of huge steel doors which will slide open to allow the rocket to take off. The men are standing in the f/g, dwarfed by the booster rocket as it towers almost to the ceiling. About three quarters of the way up the booster rocket we can see the L-15 Space Shuttle. The shuttle and the rocket shouldn't look too futuristic; there should be a definite air of clunky, post-war design to them. A complicated maze of stairs and walkways surrounds the rocket, giving access to the engines etc. In the b/g, men in white coats work on complex engine parts. It's a hive of activity as men scramble up and down the stairs. Watching over it all is Herbert Von Rhine, an ex-Nazi scientist. He's in his fifties, grey hair, but he's a huge brute of a man, just as big as Grusov. He stands in the middle distance, his back to us, looking up at the shuttle.

NO DIALOGUE

PANEL 2
Close shot of the four crew members gazing up in awe at the shuttle. They've never seen anything like it.

BROWN: YE GODS!

PANEL 3
A wide shot as Von Rhine stands in front of the men, his hands are in the pockets of his white lab jacket. Jackington makes the introductions. Everyone but Jackington and Von Rhine seems to be on edge.

JACKINGTON: GENTLEMEN, ALLOW ME TO INTRODUCE YOU TO DR. HERBERT VON RHINE. DESIGNER OF THE L-15 SPACE SHUTTLE.

PANEL 4
Close on Von Rhine. He smiles at us - an evil, slimy smile that makes us want to kick his face in.

VON RHINE: SO, MY FRIENDS . . . WHAT DO YOU THINK OF HER?

LUNA
27

PAGE THIRTY-NINE
Five panels

PANEL 1
We're in a large storage room, somewhere deep underground. The b/g is full of wooden crates and stacks of storage boxes. Lavoisier holds a Thompson M1A1 machine gun – it's been modified to fire on the lunar surface. He holds the gun awkwardly, as though he is afraid that it might explode in his face.

CAPTION: SEPTEMBER 16TH

LAVOISIER: BUT I AM A MAN OF SCIENCE, I HAVE NO NEED FOR AUTOMATIC WEAPONS.

PANEL 2
Brown is facing Lavoisier, he's grinning. Brown holds the same model of gun in his right hand. He cocks the mechanism.

BROWN: HA! THAT'S WHAT EVERYONE SAYS . . .

BROWN: UNTIL THE MERDE HITS THE FAN.

PANEL 3
An aerial shot of our four adventurers and Spears. They're standing in a wide circle. Lots of storage boxes behind them.

SPEARS: SOME OF YOU WILL ALREADY KNOW THE THOMPSON, HELL OF A WEAPON. THESE HAVE BEEN MODIFIED BY THE SCIENCE BODS. THEY SHOULD WORK IN THE LUNAR ENVIRONMENT.

GRUSOV: SHOULD?

PANEL 4
We're looking past Lavoisier as Spears opens one of the boxes. Inside we can see several rectangular blocks of plastic explosive, labeled COMPOSITION B+. Lavoisier is worried that with all the explosives and weaponry on board, the shuttle might explode.

LAVOISIER: PERSONALLY, I JUST HOPE THAT WE DO NOT EXPLODE INTO A MILLION PIECES AS SOON AS THE JET ENGINES IGNITE.

PANEL 5
Brown is now holding the machine gun in his left hand; he's just pulled out a vicious looking bowie knife with his right. He's had it hidden somewhere about his person up until now. It has a bone handle, the blade is about six inches long and it has been well used but equally well looked after. He holds the knife out to show it to Lavoisier. Brown is grinning but he's not joking around here, he's deadly serious.

BROWN: I'LL SECOND THAT.

BROWN: AND IF THE GUNS AND EXPLOSIVES DON'T WORK . . . IT'S ALWAYS ADVISABLE TO HAVE A BACK UP PLAN!

BROWN: . . . WHAT!!!

LUNA 39

THEY WANT OUR
PLANET!
AND EVERYTHING ON IT
SOTTE
BUY EARTH BONDS TODAY!
KEEP THE SLIME FROM OUR SHORE

**Above: Jim's first alien concept sketches.**

**Left: Anti-alien propaganda poster by Matt Soffe.**

**Matt Soffe ekes out a living in the North West of England, in a house without right angles that he shares with his girlfriend and cat. See more of his output at mygrimmbrother.blogspot.co.uk**

**Martin Hayes** lives in Ireland. His short stories have been published in magazines such as Nature, Flurb, and Innsmouth Free Press, while his comic work has appeared in the pages of Futurequake, Wasted, and Overload, among others. He is the author of the graphic biography Aleister Crowley - Wandering the Waste. You can see what he's been up to at www.paroneiria.com

**Jim Boswell** lives in Manchester, UK. He has worked as a freelance illustrator/cartoonist for over 20 years; his comic work includes stints on Starship Troopers for Markosia, a monthly strip for the kids football magazine KiCK! and work for various small press publications. His website can be found at www.jimmibo.co.uk

www.ingramcontent.com/pod-product-compliance
Ingram Content Group UK Ltd.
Pitfield, Milton Keynes, MK11 3LW, UK
UKHW061953290726
14090UKWH00021B/1203

9 781909 276024